ASSAULT ON TUY DONG

Gerber yelled to his men, "Keep moving. Watch your flanks. Watch your flanks."

More firing began, all around him. Some of it was incoming. He could see the green tracers. Shooting from the hip, he tried to put four shots into the muzzle flash of the enemy weapon. He heard a shout but couldn't tell if he had hit the target or merely irritated it.

The one thing that Gerber feared most was happening. The men with Fetterman were diving for available cover. Fetterman saw it too and knew what it meant. They would be pinned down and overrun. He turned, saw a VC soldier, and dropped him with a single rifle shot. Then he spun and kicked at one of the Vietnamese, trying to get him moving.

To Minh, he shouted, "If they don't move, we leave them."

THE SCORPION SQUAD *series from Pinnacle Books*

THE SCORPION SQUAD #3

CHOPPER COMMAND
Eric Helm

PINNACLE BOOKS **NEW YORK**

Dedicated to the officers and men of the 187th Assault Helicopter Company (Crusaders) Tay Ninh, and to the officers and men of the 116th Assault Helicopter Company (Hornets) Cu Chi, Republic of Vietnam, 1968-1969.

THE SCORPION SQUAD #3: CHOPPER COMMAND

Copyright © 1985 by Eric Helm

An original Pinnacle Books edition, published for the first time anywhere.

First printing/March 1985

ISBN: 0-523-42434-5

Can. ISBN: 0-523-43296-8

Printed in the United States of America

PINNACLE BOOKS, INC.
1430 Broadway
New York, New York 10018

THE A-TEAM

CAPTAIN MACK GERBER	American A-team Commander
FIRST LIEUTENANT JONATHAN BROMHEAD	Executive Officer
MASTER SERGEANT ANTHONY B. FETTERMAN	Team Sergeant
SERGEANT FIRST CLASS IAN McMILLAN	Senior Medical Specialist
STAFF SERGEANT THOMAS JEFFERSON WASHINGTON	Medical Specialist
STAFF SERGEANT SULLY SMITH	Demolitions Expert
STAFF SERGEANT MILES CLARKE	Demolitions Expert
STAFF SERGEANT GALVIN BOCKER	Communications Specialist
SERGEANT SEAN CAVANAUGH (wounded and in hospital)	Communications Specialist
SERGEANT FIRST-CLASS JUSTIN "BOOM-BOOM" TYME	Light Weapons Specialist
SERGEANT FIRST-CLASS STEVEN KITTREDGE	Heavy Weapons Specialist
SERGEANT FIRST-CLASS DEREK KEPLER	Intelligence Specialist

PROLOGUE

The seven-man VC propaganda cadre had entered the village in the early afternoon, explaining that they would be interviewing everyone during the next few hours. They would talk about the new war that had come to the region and why the imperialist Americans had invaded their homeland. They expected nothing in return, other than the courtesy of a small outdoor meeting, a little food, and some time.

None of the villagers knew that there was nearly an entire company of NVA* regulars surrounding them. This was for the protection of the cadre and to ensure that the imperialist Americans didn't sneak in to break up the performance.

That night everyone was forced to be at the meeting. The fire in the center of Cai Thoi lit the area well. The VC knew that American patrols and American

---

*A glossary appears on page 213.

aircraft would not be working nearby at the time. And the ARVN never went out at night.

Now the tone of the VC cadre changed. During the afternoon they had been kind, listening to the complaints of the villagers, telling them that the Americans had to be driven from their homeland and filling their heads with visions of Vietnamese history. At the evening meeting, they began accusing everyone of collaborating with the Americans. Then they dragged the village chief, tied hand and foot, to the center of the hamlet and accused him of taking money from the Americans and selling out his people.

While he watched, the VC pulled his wife to a pole planted near the fire and tied her to it. With a metal rod, they beat her senseless. When she was unconscious, they cut her throat, laughing as blood spurted down her body to pool at her feet.

Next they found the two teenage daughters of the chief. The girls had their hands bound behind them and were forced to kneel in front of the cadre. Slowly, their clothes were cut from their bodies, until they were naked and bleeding from a dozen wounds where the knives had cut too deep. Both girls were whimpering, but neither had yet said a word.

They were pulled to their feet. The leader of the cadre, a muscular man of forty with slicked-back hair, pushed the younger of the girls toward a hootch nearby. He forced her inside and then made her kneel in front of him as he unbuckled his pants, exposing himself. She tried to look away, but he grabbed her head in both of his hands, pulling her face into his crotch and telling her that her cooperation might just save the lives of her father and her sister.

As the VC leader finished with her, she no longer

felt anything, except a kind of deadness inside. Her salvation was that she had saved the lives of her father and sister, and surely they would forgive her.

The VC leader jerked her to her feet and led her back outside. He displayed her to the villagers, letting them see the evidence of his power that was still on her face.

Finally, she was stood next to her sister so that ropes could be tied tightly around their knees. They wouldn't be able to run, but would be able to stand. With a knife, he slashed them, cutting their chests, breasts, and stomachs. The wounds were not deep. Only painful.

After nearly thirty minutes of this, the man moved away from the two blood-drenched girls. He mounted a wooden platform that had been placed in front of them and began the lecture. His speech was long and filled with references to collaborating with the hated American enemy and assisting the puppet troops of the corrupt and illegal government in Saigon. The enemies of the people would be punished by the Viet Cong San. The true seat of government, of all of Vietnam, was with Ho Chi Minh in Hanoi. Those who defied it would die horribly.

When he finished, he stepped from the platform and walked behind the two shaking girls. Each time one of them had fallen to her knees or showed signs of fainting, the cadre had forced her to her feet or revived her. For a moment he looked at them. Dried blood covered them from the neck to the thighs. There were hundreds of minor wounds on their upper bodies. If left alone, the cuts would quickly heal, leaving little physical evidence that anything had ever happened to them.

Now he forced the girls to their knees, facing their father, who was still tied and unhurt. The VC leader moved close to the older of the girls, quietly drew his pistol, and shot her once in the base of the skull. She pitched forward without a sound, the top of her head missing and her blood and brains leaking into the red dirt of the center of the village.

The other girl screamed as she stared at her dead sister. She felt the barrel of the pistol against her own head and heard the hammer pulled back. She twisted around, trying to see the man behind her. She knew that the man had lied to her, and her eyes grew wide with fright. She screamed continuously as she waited for death.

The VC leader looked at her and smiled. His eyes held hers and she knew that she was going to die. But instead of pulling the trigger, he stepped in front of her and kicked her in the stomach, knocking her to her side. She lost consciousness.

Instead of killing her, he told the villagers that the VC were merciful. They knew that the girl was the unwilling dupe of her capitalist father. She was an innocent pawn in a power struggle that she could not comprehend. The man moved to her father and, using a long, sharp knife handed to him, slit the man from the groin to the breastbone, spilling his intestines out. Then, as a final sign of his contempt, he stepped on the entrails, grinding them into the dirt with the heel of his boot as he spit on the dying man.

He finished, telling them that the merciful VC were now going to leave. They expected help from the villagers of Cai Thoi. They would want to know when the Americans moved through their hamlet, where they camped, where they patrolled, and what they did. Sometimes, they would expect food and shelter, and an occasional recruit. If the villagers complied, the VC would protect them. If they didn't, they would be punished. The VC were going to leave the younger daughter alive as a reminder of their mercy and with the hope that the now-enlightened villagers would be able to teach her the error of her ways.

By dawn, the VC cadre had faded into Cambodia where they would be safe. The majority of the company of soldiers who had guarded them went with them. A few of the men were left behind to watch the villagers to make sure they didn't try to contact the Americans.

CHAPTER 1 ————————————

SPECIAL FORCES CAMP A-555,
MEKONG RIVER REGION,
RVN

It was long after dawn when Sergeant First-Class Derek Kepler and Staff Sergeant Sully Smith reached the outer perimeter wire. They had been in the field for just over thirty-six hours, following a Viet Cong cadre of propaganda specialists, the task complicated by the company of North Vietnamese soldiers who were acting as guard for the cadre. The Americans had had to stay concealed as the cadre, and the majority of the North Vietnamese, slipped back across the border into Cambodia.

At first light, Kepler and Smith crawled away from their hiding place, passing within a few feet of a sleeping NVA soldier. Once out of the area, they rushed back to the camp so they could report. On the way, Kepler felt the budding of an idea. By the time they reached the outer wire, it was nearly in full flower.

Captain Mack Gerber, the twenty-nine-year-old CO of the Special Forces A-team, met them at the gate.

7

He hadn't liked the idea of a two-man patrol, but there had seemed to be no other way to run it. Two men to slip up on the VC, listen to their propaganda, and then fade back into the jungle. The local troops couldn't be counted on not to take the opportunity to kill the VC. There were those who would have been a good risk, but Kepler wanted it kept simple.

As Kepler stepped through the gate, Gerber said, "You get what you were after?"

"Yes sir. Sure did." He looked around cautiously. "I can brief you on it now, if you like."

Gerber stared at the unshaven, tired-looking man. "Why don't you get something to eat and wash up. I'll be in my hootch when you've had a chance to relax."

Kepler and Smith turned, heading to the team house to drop their equipment and get some breakfast. Around them the camp was already awake and working on various projects. Kepler could see that Kittredge had succeeded in finding two more fifty-caliber machine guns. They were being sited so that they could cover either end of the runway located in the center of the camp.

For a moment, Gerber watched the two men walk off. There had been something in Kepler's eyes that he couldn't understand. Something that looked as old and tired as he felt, but something that also looked disgusted. It was a lot to be reading into the expression of a twenty-six-year-old man who had just spent a couple of days in the field.

Back at his hootch, Gerber sat down at the makeshift desk built out of bamboo and ammo crates. It wasn't as pretty as the monstrosity that General Billy Joe Crinshaw had in Saigon, but it was functional.

For thirty minutes he pushed the papers around the top of it, supposedly reading reports about the status of the camp's projects, but he remembered nothing from them. He kept thinking about that strange look that was on Kepler's face.

Finished with breakfast, Kepler and Smith walked over to the captain's hootch and knocked on the frame of the door before they went in. Gerber waved them into the steel folding chairs that sat in front of the desk and said, "Okay, what happened?"

"We found them," said Kepler, "almost right away, and just where we thought they would be. Our information on that point was very good. And they weren't making any real effort to hide themselves. I guess that cadre leader figured that a company of hardcore regulars could take anything we could throw at them."

"They were hardcore? You sure?"

"Captain, I was as close to them as you are to me and I can tell an NVA uniform when I see one. These guys were dressed in green uniforms, not black pajamas. They were North Vietnamese."

"I wasn't doubting your word, Derek, it's just that I'm surprised that they're working out here."

"I'm not, particularly, Captain," said the intelligence sergeant. "It makes good sense. We beat off a pretty big attack, so they send in a propaganda team to explain why we're still here."

Gerber got up and walked to a wall cabinet. "Either of you guys want a touch of the Beams?"

Kepler looked at his watch. "I usually don't have a drink before five."

"It's after ten now," said Gerber with a smile. He

poured a shot for each of them. Turning back to face them, he said, "Go ahead, Derek."

Kepler launched into a detailed account of what they had seen, describing graphically the scene when the VC executed the village chief and most of his family. He also said that the cadre lost most of the village when they did that. Kepler could tell by the revulsion on their faces as they watched the young girl and then her father die. He also described the uniforms of the cadre and its bodyguard, the weapons they carried, and the positions of each of them.

When he finished, Gerber said, "Nothing you could do to stop it?"

"What do you want, Captain?" Kepler said emotionally. "There were nearly a hundred and fifty NVA and only two of us."

"Take it easy, Derek. I had to ask the question. What are your recommendations?"

Now it was Kepler's turn to feel uncomfortable. He looked at Smith, who had remained silent during most of the debriefing. Finally he said, "Well, it would seem to me that the surviving daughter would be perfect as an intelligence asset. The VC have made themselves a strong enemy in her."

"Isn't that a little bit callous?" asked Gerber.

"I know how you feel, Captain, but I think we have an opportunity here that we won't want to waste. That VC political cadre will be coming back into the area, and if we can get enough people out there watching for us, we might be able to capture them."

Gerber shook his head. "I don't know."

"Just listen, sir, then decide. We'll need the support of helicopters to make it work because we'll need a fast reaction time. And we'll need a lot of people out there to help look, but if we can get it, we can capture them."

"What are you talking about?"

Kepler stood up and paced toward the door, then back to his chair and sat down. "Simply, sir, we keep the people watching and when we learn where the propaganda cadre is going to be, we launch a quick reaction strike using the helicopters to airlift a strike force into the area."

Gerber leaned back, steepled his fingers under his chin, and said, "It's going to be a real coordination nightmare, not to mention the fact that I don't think we could get the helicopters here fast enough. Besides, you guys got there in a couple of hours. Why do we need a bunch of helicopters?"

"I thought about that sir. The thing is, we weren't alerted until late in the day and had to rush to get there. If we had tried to take a company with us, we would have scared them off. They would have seen us coming. You know how the VC grapevine works."

"That still doesn't get your choppers here in time."

Kepler sort of laughed. "It does if we could have them standing by on the airstrip."

"No way. Crinshaw would have a fit."

"Yes sir, but you could tell him that Charlie is still operating with impunity here. It would be a way of stopping him. A mission that should make the Saigon warriors happy. I'm sure that our people in Nha Trang would approve."

"You take a lot for granted."

"Yes sir. But you can do it. Think about what it would mean to us. First, we manage to throw back the VC assault on the camp and then we capture their propaganda team. It would make quite a dent in the myth of Charlie's ability and invulnerability. And give Crinshaw a nice bone to throw to the Saigon press corps."

"I still don't see why you want the choppers here," said Gerber, shaking his head.

"Quick reaction. We could get our people into the field, anywhere in our AO in a matter of minutes.

"I suppose there are a number of things we could do with the choppers while they're here. Might help us get things settled down a little. Run some psyops and aerial recon."

"Then you'll try sir?"

"It won't hurt to propose the idea to Bates. All he can say is no."

"That's right, Captain. All he can say is no. Crinshaw's the only one who can say yes."

"One final question," said Gerber. "What about that chief's teenage daughter?"

"I thought that once this is over, we might be able to find a spot for her in Saigon. Surely someone in the embassy, or at MACV headquarters could get her a job. Maybe see that she gets some schooling. I mean, if she helps us, we should help her."

"Okay. You get your report written up and I'll take it to Bates to see what he says. If we can sell him, we might be able to slip it past Crinshaw. Make an extra copy to get to the people up in Nha Trang. Include in that your recommendations about setting up the agent network." He thought for a minute and then said, "Don't say anything about the chief's daughter."

"Why not?"

"For one thing, we don't have her recruited, and

for another, I don't want too many people to know about it. I'm just not comfortable using someone that young, especially one who has just been through the experience she has. I want you to handle that very carefully."

"When do you think you'll go to Saigon, sir?"

"I don't know about that. I'll want to take a little longer look at this."

"I'll have something for you this afternoon, sir."

After Kepler and Smith left, Gerber sat in his room, tapping a pencil against the edge of his desk, staring into the distance. He, and his team, had been back at the camp for just over three weeks, replacing Henderson and his team. Henderson had made several modifications, not all of which Gerber liked. But with some of the revolts in strike companies in other camps, Gerber had decided that he would let the changes stand. Saigon was always trying to move strike companies from one base to another, so there was no guarantee that the companies he had now would remain at the camp. So he left the secret demolition charges in place under the major crew-served weapons. If, during an assault, the crew switched allegiance, Gerber could now blow them up. Supposedly only Gerber and the other A-team members knew about the explosives, but he suspected that Lieutenant Minh, the camp commander and head of the Luc Luong Dac Biet assigned there, knew of them also. Knowing Minh as he did, Gerber wouldn't have been too surprised to find the Vietnamese camp commander had his own demolition network.

Henderson's intelligence NCO had begun the

building of a network of agents, something that Kepler would have done had they not been so busy trying to get the camp completed before the VC could storm it. Now, Kepler had a list of ten men and women who would pass information to the Green Berets in exchange for money, food supplies, or favors.

Kepler had met each of the agents, usually at a rendezvous in the jungle so that the other Vietnamese wouldn't become suspicious. The risk of betrayal and ambush had been high, but the meetings had gone without a hitch. Once that was done, Kepler began trying to recruit more.

He also spent a couple of days in the field, building a map of the local area, coloring in the suspected locations of VC bases, where abandoned bases were located, and suspected routes of travel. He was also trying to put together an accurate list of VC agents around the camp. He wasn't having a lot of luck, but he was having some.

Gerber had, in keeping with standing orders, told Kepler to prepare a list of everything that he was doing so that they could advise Special Forces headquarters in Nha Trang. Kepler had argued about that, afraid that his agents and ideas would be compromised, but orders were orders.

In the early evening, as the sun set, Gerber toured the camp, looking at the defenses. Henderson, during his temporary stay, had abandoned the idea of an alert from just before sunset to just after because there had been no hostile activity all during the time he had been there. Since Charlie hadn't even bothered to drop mortars, Gerber let that ride too.

He was on the north wall, looking at the almost

unending field of elephant grass. The sun was low, touching the horizon, and Gerber was watching the waving grass when he heard the tell-tale whump of a mortar. Seconds later it hit, on the east perimeter, between the third and fourth strands of wire.

A minute later, from another location, a second round was fired. It didn't even hit the perimeter wire. And three minutes after that, there was a third round from a third location. It landed outside the perimeter too.

Since the three shots had come from three different locations, there wasn't a chance of finding the tubes or the enemy mortarmen. The fact that the VC would be so careful meant that they respected the ability of the men in the camp but felt they had to do something to let everyone know they were around. Gerber couldn't help laughing. It was such a poor showing that he didn't even bother with an alert.

That night, at the team meeting, Gerber announced part of Kepler's plan. "What he wants to do is organize a quick reaction team to hit the VC as they begin one of their propaganda meetings. The force would stand by near the flight line and would go out as the agents reported in. The primary objective would be to capture the cadre." He finished outlining the procedure and said, "Any questions or opinions from the rest of you?"

"Where do you plan to park the helicopters, if we get them?" asked Anthony Fetterman, the team sergeant. He was the oldest and smallest of the Green Berets, but he was also the toughest. He was a veteran of both World War II and Korea who never needed to give an order twice.

"Hadn't thought about it."

"If I may," said Lieutenant Bromhead, the executive officer. "The best place would be on the east side of the runway, near the north wall. We could throw up a couple of revetments easily, and we have the space there. Anyone trying to approach the camp from the outside has to come the longest distance over open ground."

"And," said Kepler, "they'll be close to our quarters and the tents the pilots will use. Allow a quicker reaction time."

"How many and who goes on the reaction team?" asked Sergeant Tyme, the light weapons specialist. He was among the youngest of the American Special Forces men, having entered the army right out of high school.

"Again," answered Gerber, "that's still in the planning stage. It depends how many helicopters we get, if any."

"What about ammo for the helicopters?" asked Tyme.

"They can bring their own."

Galvin Bocker, the senior communications NCO asked, "What about radio communications?"

"Shouldn't be a problem. Everything we have is compatible with their systems." Gerber held up his hands and said, "Everything we're going over here is really trivia. There hasn't been one question that doesn't deal with a fairly minor aspect of this idea."

"Okay, Captain," said Fetterman. "How about refueling the helicopters? They're either going to have to do it at some other base and fly here, burning up that fuel, or we're going to have to find a way of refueling them here."

Gerber nodded. "Good. Hadn't thought of that. That's the kind of thing I've been looking for. Listen, why don't each of you write down the problems you think we'll encounter, and before I go to Saigon to pitch this to Colonel Bates, we'll see if there is anything that will really foul this up."

Late the next morning, Gerber had the various reports, and the only real problem that had cropped up was the helicopters' refueling brought up by Fetterman. But Fetterman had offered two solutions for it. One was to bring in a large fuel truck to top off the tanks of the helicopters. The other was to install a fuel bladder. Of the two, Fetterman suggested the truck because it wouldn't be the target that a large fuel storage bladder would be. Of course, that presented a new problem. Driving the truck in from outside.

By noon he had set up an appointment with Bates for the next day. Since the communications with Saigon weren't secure, Gerber could not mention the nature of the plan, only that they had an idea that might make some difference in the war effort.

CHAPTER 2 _____

Warrant Officer Charles Ramsey sat on the troop seat in the back of his UH-1D helicopter and looked at the bullet hole in the windshield. Each time he saw it, he became angry all over again. How could they win the war by running from the enemy? A couple of rounds fired at the flight, and they aborted the mission to run away. Ramsey couldn't understand it, and he didn't like it.

His copilot, Warrant Officer Fred Chrisman, lay on the floor of the cargo compartment, using a bullet-resistant, ceramic chest protector for a pillow. He was asleep, having heard all that he cared to about the chicken-shit ARVN troops that they had to work with. He didn't care that they had aborted the landing while a new airstrike or artillery barrage reprepared the LZ. He didn't care about much of anything, except sleeping, eating, and writing letters to a girl back in the World, who never wrote in return.

Ramsey leaned forward and kicked the top of the

19

chicken plate, waking Chrisman. "Why don't you go talk to lead. See what they're doing."

"They'll let us know when it's time," said Chrisman, opening one eye so that he could see Ramsey.

"Do it anyway."

Chrisman sat up, leaned over so that he could see the clock on the side of the instrument panel, and then leaped out of the helicopter. As he stared toward the lead aircraft, the pilot got out and signaled the others by waving his arm over his head.

Chrisman said, "We're supposed to crank."

Ramsey, as aircraft commander, got into the left side of the helicopter, although the right side was set up as the AC's seat. The visibility was better on the left side. He strapped in and let Chrisman start the engine.

Minutes later they were airborne, heading toward an old French fort to pick up the ARVN. The loads were separated into squads of eight men each, and they landed next to one group, armed with BARs and M-1s. The ARVN scrambled aboard the helicopters, and within a couple of seconds they lifted off.

The flight orbited at the IP for several minutes as the last of the artillery rounds hit the ground, sending fountains of dark earth into the air. Over the radio, they heard, "Last rounds on the way."

Lead broke toward the LZ as the final salvo of artillery shells landed dead center. Setting up the approach from the south, lead began a rapid descent that would use the trees as a shield. When they were less than half a klick out, they began taking sporadic small arms fire from a small hamlet on the right.

Overhead, the C and C said, "You have negative suppression. You are not to fire into the village."

From the right, the intensity of the fire increased. Negative suppression meant they weren't supposed to shoot back, even if they could identify a target. The rationale for not shooting into the village was that they didn't want to turn the villagers into VC. Ramsey thought that it might be too late for that.

Then they were over the trees, screened from the village, and fast approaching the landing zone. Gunships on each side of the flight rolled in, hitting the treelines on both sides with rockets. In front of them, a third gunship dived from overhead, heading toward the center of the LZ. Ramsey's machine guns, firing forward, were raking the ground. As he swooped low, a smoke grenade dropped out of the back, marking the touch down point for the flight leader.

Just as the two gunships on the sides of the flight broke left and right, firing erupted from the trees. But instead of the intense shooting of the first attempt, during which Ramsey had lost part of his windshield, this was spotty and uncoordinated. Most of the bullets were missing the aircraft, now sitting on the ground.

Ramsey sat holding the cyclic and collective, waiting for the crew chief to tell him that the ARVN had gotten out. When he heard nothing, he turned to look over his shoulder and saw them all sitting there, cowering behind the little protection offered in the cargo compartment.

"Hey, Wong, shove these fuckers out of here. We're going to get shot to hell."

But Wong, the crew chief, had already dropped

the handle of his M-60 machine gun and was trying to throw the reluctant ARVN out of the helicopter.

"Lead, why are you still on the ground?" asked the C and C over the radio.

"Troops are refusing to unass."

In the back of Ramsey's helicopter, the door gunner had also climbed forward and was trying to throw the ARVN out the door. Wong was doing the same, and although the ARVN weren't fighting the Americans, as soon as one was tossed out, he scrambled back on board.

"Sir," said Wong, "could you pick up to a hover so these jerks can't get back on."

Ramsey sucked in a little pitch, raising the aircraft off its skids so that it was hanging in the air about four feet above the ground. Wong was screaming at the top of his voice, threatening to shoot the ARVN if they didn't get off.

Firing around them increased because nearly all the door gunners in the flight were now busy with the ARVN. One round hit near Wong's head, ripping through the soundproofing and showering the ARVN with fragments. Suddenly, almost as if they realized that they were making good targets in the helicopters, the ARVN were fighting each other to get out. Wong leaped back to his gun and opened fire on the treeline.

Over the radio, "Lead, you're down with ten and unloaded. Fire on the right and left."

"Lead's on the go."

As one, the flight rolled over, picking up airspeed as they flew toward the treeline at the front of the LZ. They all lifted into a climb.

"You're out with ten."

"Roger. Come up in a staggered trail."

"Lead, head for home. That should be it."

On the ground, the ARVN, left alone with only four American advisers, were now, at least, shooting at the VC. Two of the Americans were throwing grenades, while a third, using a radio, was directing the fire of the three gunships that had remained on station. He was also trying to get an airstrike in. Not that it mattered, because the VC, having inflicted what damage they could, were already trying to break contact and fade into the jungle.

Back at Bien Hoa, Ramsey was livid. First there was the go-around, then the second assault where they sat on the ground trying to convince the ARVN to get out. The South Vietnamese didn't want to fight, didn't know how to fight, and were just as likely to shoot up the helicopters as were the enemy. He nearly screamed at Chrisman, claiming that he would volunteer for anything as long as it didn't involve the ARVN. They weren't worth the powder it would take to blow them all to hell.

At Special Forces Camp A-555, Sergeant Kepler was organizing a patrol to head out to Cai Thoi, the village that had been visited by the VC propaganda cadre. He wanted to talk to the girl whose parents and sister had been murdered but was afraid that it was too soon after the deaths. That the Vietnamese would misunderstand what he wanted.

And then he realized that he was afraid that they would understand all too well what he wanted. They would see this as just one more invasion of their privacy. First the VC kill the village chief and most of his family, then the Americans come to take the only survivor.

It wasn't a task that Kepler enjoyed, but it was one that was necessary. The Special Forces men needed the help, and if Kepler could learn more about the activities of the propaganda cadre, he might be able to stop them. In fact, if he could learn more about any of the VC in the area, he might be able to rid the whole zone of them. But first he had to talk to the girl.

Sully Smith found Kepler sitting alone, cleaning his weapon one last time. He said, "You have everyone you need for your patrol?"

"Could always use one more," said Kepler, not looking up.

"Well, I wouldn't mind the opportunity. Not much happening around here right now, other than planning for the helicopter revetments, which is a bit premature."

Kepler set his cleaning rag aside and looked down the barrel of the rifle. He picked up the rod and thrust it through once more. "I thought you had learned to never volunteer."

"Yeah." Smith laughed. "Never volunteer."

Like everyone else in the Special Forces, he was a volunteer, who had originally volunteered for jump training. Then for unconventional warfare training. And then for Vietnam. In fact, volunteering was nearly a way of life in the Special Forces.

"Thought we would move out just after dark. That way we should reach the edge of the ville about one or two in the morning, and have several hours to watch it before we go in. We have to be very careful."

"Which of the strikers are you taking?"

"Hadn't thought much about it. I'd like to take Minh, but I suppose, with Captain Gerber in Saigon, Minh should stay here. Probably ask him to assign us a couple."

"Then you're not going to ask Sergeant Krung?" asked Smith.

"Thought I'd limit the patrol to ethnic Viets and avoid the interracial problems. I'm not sure, but I think most of the lowland Vietnamese hate Krung's hill people."

"Great. Let's make the world safe for democracy, but only if you happen to belong to the right ethnic group."

While Ramsey and Chrisman complained about the ARVN and Kepler and Smith worried about the ethnic makeup of their patrol, Mack Gerber sat in Lieutenant Colonel Alan Bates's office in Saigon, trying to explain why he wanted five helicopters and crews. Gerber had spent a lot of time in the Spartan office. Bates had an old metal desk, two chairs, and a couple of army prints depicting great battles. The plywood floor was dirty and a fan overhead did little more than stir up the dust. The one window was open.

Bates had been sitting with his back more or less to Gerber. He had his feet propped up on an open desk drawer and was looking out the window. When Gerber finally said that he wanted five helicopters, Bates dropped his feet to the floor. He stared at Gerber. "You want what?"

"Five helicopters."

"There is no way in hell that General Crinshaw is going to approve assigning five helicopters to you."

"Maybe he will if we tell him the right story."

Bates stared at the young captain. He knew that Gerber had received his commission through ROTC, but he had been to some of the finest schools the military had to offer including the one at the Special Warfare Center. Now he wondered if all the training had really had an impact. Besides, Gerber's degree was in botany. Not exactly an area of importance to the military.

But Gerber did look the part of a Special Forces officer. He was tall, had brown hair and blue eyes, and looked mean. He also studied military history and had often said that he was basically fighting the Indian Wars all over, and as soon as the brass in Saigon realized that, they could get onto the business of fighting the war.

"Okay, why don't you tell me this plan?"

"To begin, maybe I should tell a few facts obtained at high risk by the intelligence specialist."

Bates laughed. "Save the commercial for General Crinshaw. I know all about your intelligence specialist. Isn't he the one who showed up drunk, wearing a nurse's uniform?"

"Yes sir, he sure did. The full uniform including stockings and a bra," said Gerber, smiling.

"You ever find out why?"

"No sir. He just said it was necessary to secure the 90mm recoilless rifle he had with him. I figured if he could come back with a ninety every time, I'd buy him a nurse's uniform myself."

"What about the five helicopters?"

"As I say, Sergeant Kepler has learned that there is a VC propaganda cadre operating near our camp. From what he's put together—and admittedly, some of it is speculation—they are either North Vietnamese, or have been trained by the North Vietnamese. They are the enemy's response to our presence and the fact that the VC didn't eliminate the camp as they had claimed they would.''

''That still doesn't get me to the five helicopters.''

''In a way it does. Kepler is establishing a network of locals who will give us information on the movements of the VC. Much of the information will be of an extremely perishable nature. That is, the VC are here now but will be gone tomorrow. Information on the cadre will be even more transient. We have to strike when we have the chance, and the only way to do that is to use helicopters.''

''All you have to do is coordinate that through us,'' said Bates.

''Oh come on,'' said Gerber. ''You don't believe that. You know that we have to lay the missions on two days in advance, and then you're liable to get preempted.''

Bates whirled around so that he was facing Gerber. ''I'll grant you that.''

''If we have them at the camp, we could be airborne in thirty minutes. We could hit the VC before they had a chance to react.''

''I can tell you right now that the biggest objection is going to be that we can't afford to have five helicopters sitting around for days without anything to do.''

''But that's no problem. Since we don't know where the cadre will be, we'll have to run normal patrols. We could use the choppers to put our people out and to pick them. There are recon flights we need to make. A thousand things that we could use them for."

"What about refueling?"

"They could refuel at any of the airfields around and fly back to our camp. We'll need a fuel truck, maybe two, to top off the tanks after they refuel off station. That way we can keep a full fuel load on the choppers."

"There are a hundred logistical problems. Billeting the flight crews. Food. Ammo."

Gerber interrupted. "We have a couple of general purpose tents we could erect for them. Food might be only C-rations, but they'll have all they can eat. And ammo. When they refuel they can pick up the ammo they need."

"You seem to have worked out the details."

"We've tried to anticipate the problems, but if I can get with someone from an aviation company, we could finish the planning."

For a moment Bates just shook his head. "I don't know. I don't think we'll be able to find anyone willing to do it."

"You could check, though."

"I suppose so. I'll have to clear this through our headquarters at Nha Trang. They'll have to alert Crinshaw and he's going to hit the roof."

"How soon?"

"Look, Mack, you've already had one big victory out there. That should impress the people."

Now Gerber sat up. "You know that military successes are like last week's football victories. They're forgotten when the ones this week are announced. I've already heard rumors around my area about the Go Den massacre. The VC took the whole camp with

no trouble at all. The one survivor has talked to a lot
of people."

"What's that mean?"

"Only that the people know about the Go Den
failure and that the VC have now walked right into
Cai Thoi and killed the chief. We have got to prove
to them that they will be safe if they side with us."

"All right. I'll see what I can do." Bates privately
figured that he wouldn't be able to find an aviation
unit that would volunteer.

"Thanks, Colonel. I knew you'd help."

In Bates's outer office, Gerber picked up the field
phone and tried to place a call to Nha Trang so that
he could talk to Lieutenant Karen Morrow. She was
an air-force flight nurse Gerber had known since just
before the VC had tried to capture his camp. He had
even managed to take her on an R and R with him,
although he had been recalled early.

He got through to the evac hospital with no problems and even managed to get switched to the ward
where Morrow worked. From there it went down
hill.

"I'm sorry, Captain, but the lieutenant left earlier
this afternoon."

"Do you know where she might be?"

"Yes sir, I sure do. She, and three other nurses,
were sent down to Saigon for a couple days to fill in.
They have had some kind of infection down there
and a lot of the medical people are sick."

Gerber pulled the phone away from his ear for a
moment and stared at it in disbelief. "She's here in
Saigon?"

"Yes sir. Been there for a couple of hours now, I would imagine."

"Do you know how to find her here?"

"Shouldn't be that hard. Just go over to the hospital on the airbase and you should find her."

"Thanks," said Gerber. He slammed the receiver down and looked at the sergeant sitting behind the desk there. "How do I promote a jeep around here?"

The sergeant, an old staff man, reached into the middle drawer of his battered desk. He pulled out a key on a giant metal tag and tossed it at Gerber. "I need it back here by midnight. You can just leave the key on the desk if there is no one around."

Gerber found the hospital easily and was told that the people from Nha Trang had been assigned somewhere on the second floor. He walked up and then wandered around until he heard someone call his name.

"Mack? Is that you?"

He turned. Karen was standing near a bright window. Her green fatigues contrasted with it, making a large dark lump that was barely recognizable as human.

"Karen?"

She rushed forward, embracing him. She looked over his shoulder, saw that there was no one around, and nibbled at his ear. "God! It's good to see you."

"Can we get out of here?" asked Gerber, holding her closely.

"Not before six. They're too shorthanded. We've got a lot to do."

He released her, looking a little disappointed. Then

he said, "How about some dinner then? Or a drink? Anything?"

She laughed at him. "Sure. Dinner. A drink. Anything. As long as it's with you."

"Lieutenant Morrow, we need you over here," called someone from behind them.

"I've got to go."

"I'll be out front at eighteen hundred waiting for you."

"I might be a couple of minutes late, so if I'm not there don't go running off."

"And where do you think I'd go? I'll be there waiting until late tomorrow morning."

"See you at six."

Back at the camp, Kepler was standing just inside of the team house, looking out the door. He turned and said to Lieutenant Bromhead, "Then you'll begin firing in fifteen minutes sir?"

"That's right. I've laid on everything from the 60mm mortars to the 106mm recoilless rifles. We'll probably also fire off a bunch of .50-caliber. You think it will help?"

"I don't know, sir. I suspect that somebody is out there watching us. If we drop a lot of stuff around here, we might get out of the wire and get to the trees along the river without Charlie knowing that we're out."

"I'll give you thirty minutes of cover. After we start, I'm going to have to call into Saigon and let them know we're shooting, in retaliation to incoming. They may order an immediate halt."

"So."

Bromhead shrugged. "I'll give you thirty minutes of covering fire. Fifteen minutes after you leave here."

"All right, sir. Most of the patrol has been gathering in small groups at the south gate for the last hour. That way Charlie won't see the patrol forming."

Kepler left the team house, picked up his gear and his rifle, and strolled to the south, along the edge of the runway. As he neared the south wall, he saw two of the strikers who were assigned to the patrol and Sergeant Smith. Kepler ignored them and walked into the bunker. There he saw four Vietnamese gunners waiting for word to begin the cover fire.

Smith followed Kepler in. "Well?"

"We go in nine minutes. You ready?"

"Of course."

"And the Vietnamese?"

"You saw the two outside. There are two more waiting in a bunker near the gate. I've run an equipment check and everything seems to be in order. We're not taking much food, only a small bag of rice, but each man has two canteens and two bandoliers of ammunition. I've got a spare compass and set of maps, but haven't marked anything on the maps."

"What about the grenades?"

"Oh, yeah. Each man has three frags. I've got two yellow smoke grenades and two red smokes. The Viet with the radio has two green smokes and two reds."

Kepler moved to the firing slit and looked out. The light had faded and with the low overcast, the ground was nearly pitch black. He stepped back as the Vietnamese gunners began loading their weapons.

"Let's go," said Smith.

Outside, they waved to the two strikers and then

walked toward the gate, keeping low. A minute later, they picked up the other two members of the patrol. At the gate, they crouched, and Kepler checked his watch as he heard the first of the mortars fire. A second later, the heavy weapons in the camp opened fire in all directions.

Kepler opened the gate and ran out, keeping his head down. The Vietnamese followed him, and Smith closed the gate before he started off.

At the outer wire, Kepler threw himself to the ground, waiting for the rest of the patrol to catch up. When they were in the grass beside him, he pointed to a clump of trees about five hundred meters to the south. They all nodded.

Kepler got to his feet and began to run in that direction. He was stepping as carefully as he could, trying to stay in the little cover that was available. It was the first time that burning off the elephant grass near the camp had been a disadvantage.

The patrol spread out, the gaps between them opening to as much as twenty meters. Kepler didn't like that, but he thought the need for speed was the primary factor. Once he reached the trees, he scouted them quickly and found no evidence that the VC had been there recently. He dived to the ground near the roots of a large palm and waited while the patrol staggered in.

In the distance he could hear the camp's weapons still firing and he glimpsed an occasional flash as a mortar round exploded. The red tracers drifted, some of them striking the ground and bouncing high into the air before they burned out. And there were the sounds of some of the .30-caliber machine guns firing as some of the Vietnamese couldn't contain themselves and had to join in the mad minute.

Kepler, breathing hard, pulled his watch out of a pocket and checked the time on the slightly luminous dial. The barrage had another five minutes. The patrol joined him, spreading out, facing all directions as security. They waited for the shooting to stop.

As the firing tapered off, Kepler whispered to Smith. "We'll hang loose here for a while and see if we can spot anything. Shouldn't take more than four or five hours to reach the village."

Morrow was more than a couple of minutes late, but when Gerber saw her, it didn't matter. She had changed out of her uniform and into a light print dress. She climbed into the open jeep, leaned over so that she could kiss him, and then said, "Where are we going?"

"I figured we could get a bite at the club." He gestured at himself. "I'm afraid that I don't have anything but fatigues with me. I didn't expect to see you here."

"The club is fine. At least they have good steaks and the price is right. Cheap."

"The club it is."

"There is one other thing," said Morrow quietly. "We have a curfew."

"You what?"

"Oh, the CO in Nha Trang wouldn't let us come down here unless we were supervised by the head nurse. We have a curfew. Have to be back by eleven."

Gerber turned and looked at her, half smiling. "You have got to be kidding. That's rather provincial."

"Yeah, but the head nurse is a colonel and she could make my life here miserable."

Gerber leaned forward and started the jeep's engine. "Well, don't worry about it; we've got about five hours, so we'll just have to make the best of it."

As they had done on the other times they had been in Saigon, they went to the Ton Son Nhut officers' club for dinner. Gerber didn't really like it. Not because it wasn't a pleasant place, but because of the kinds of people who frequented it. Most of them were chairborne commandos who had all the answers for winning the war, wiping out communism, and spreading democracy throughout the world, but who had never been to the field. They lived in air-conditioned trailers or in plush hotel suites with hot and cold running girls, and it was a bad day if they had to eat a quick, cold lunch. Then, in the evening, they congregated in the officers' club to swap stories of false war and imagined horror.

But the officers' club was the only place where Gerber could relax, at least a little. Even if the Saigon warriors didn't believe it, there were terrorists running around in downtown Saigon who were bent on assassinating Americans. The brass-hatted bureaucrats had decreed that no one was to take a firearm downtown, and Gerber just couldn't see venturing into "enemy territory" without a weapon. So, reluctantly, he drove his jeep to the officers' club, where they would take his rifle away from him at the door, but he could smuggle his pistol, under his fatigue jacket, into the dining room with him.

Without looking around, Gerber walked to the table that was the farthest from the makeshift stage, away from the huge speakers that would have done justice to a concert hall, and sat down. He stared at Karen, who was sitting next to him, and felt her knee press his thigh. He gazed into her eyes and thought, once again, that he had never seen eyes so blue.

For just a moment, she was embarrassed by the intensity of his look, but then she smiled and said, "So, how's it going?"

"Well, as you probably know if you got my last letter, they sent us back to our old camp. Pulled Henderson's team and sent them off to do something else." Gerber stopped talking and wondered if he wasn't saying too much. He thought about his words and realized that even if he had been talking to a communist agent, there was nothing in what he had said to betray anything. He had been properly vague.

Karen looked away from him, a thousand questions in her mind. She felt, just as she had felt in Australia, that there was something between them. A barrier that she couldn't cross. She knew that Gerber had returned from a mission, using an abbreviated team, but she didn't know where he had been or what he had done. She wanted to know because she wanted to share with him, but the army and the war seemed to demand that he keep part of his life separate from her.

Again, she said, "How's it going?" She wanted to give him the opening to talk, if that was what he wanted, but she didn't want to force him.

"Right now, everything is fine. We are pressing our advantage."

"Is there anything you'd like to tell me?"

"You mean other than I love you?" Gerber said it flippantly, with a smile on his face. He was attempting to divert the conversation because he knew that he couldn't tell her that he had been to North Vietnam, that he had been involved in rescuing a downed air-force pilot. That mission, in and of itself, was above reproach. It was some of the other things that had happened, the firefights with the NVA, and the evacuation on the Swift boats, that left a bad taste in his mouth. But all that was classified too highly, and although he would trust Karen with his life, he didn't trust all those around them at the moment. He didn't know who might be able to hear what he said, and it wasn't beneath the principles of the army, or the air force, to bug a couple of the tables to find out who might be speaking out of turn. So rather than tell her about his trip into the north, he just sat there, waiting for the waitress to take their order.

Karen smiled at him, ignoring what he said about love. It was what she wanted to hear, but given the circumstances and the conversation, she wasn't sure that she believed him.

After nearly half an hour, they managed to get a waitress to take their order and then it took another half hour to get the food. By the time it arrived, it was only warm, heading rapidly to cold. But for Gerber, it was better than anything he had eaten for quite a while, so he was satisfied.

After dinner, they stayed at the club, drinking Beam's straight, dancing occasionally, but mostly just sitting close to each other, talking about everything from the way Saigon must have been before the war (if there had ever really been a time when some faction of the Vietnamese wasn't fighting some other faction, or invading armies), to the inauguration of the TV station for the American forces (currently broadcasting from an aircraft orbiting overhead for

only a couple of hours a day), to President Johnson's
Gulf of Tonkin speech. Gerber looked momentarily
horrified at the mention of the Gulf of Tonkin incident,
but Karen thought nothing of it, other than that it
meant more Americans in Vietnam.

They stayed at the club until ten. Then Karen,
realizing that it was getting late, asked Gerber why
they hadn't left sooner.

He stared at her and then leaned close so that he
could whisper into her ear. "Because I didn't want
you to think that I was interested in you for only one
reason. I wanted you to know that my feelings for
you went beyond the superficial and the physical."

She turned so that she could look into his eyes and
said, "I wish we had left an hour ago."

They left the bar area of the club and entered the
entrance hallway. Off to one side, near the lock
boxes where those who had them could store their
weapons, was a dark corner. Karen dragged Gerber
toward it, pressed herself against him forcibly, and
kissed him hard, pushing her tongue into his mouth.

He responded by holding her tightly.

She broke the kiss, looked at her watch, and said,
"That's going to have to hold you. I've got to get
back."

"Damn," he said breathlessly. "I wish you wouldn't
do that and then tell me you've got to go. You could
hurt me."

Slowly, they drove back to the nurses' quarters.
They sat in the jeep for a few minutes, until the
minute hand on Karen's watch had crept dangerously
close to the twelve. She said, "I've got to report in."

*   *   *

Kepler, having waited twenty minutes, finally decided that they were alone in the area. He had heard nothing and seen nothing. There had been the scrambling of tiny claws as some of the night animals ran near them. That was all. Kepler walked around his perimeter and tapped each man on the shoulder. They fell in with him, and all began to move toward the village, staying away from the path that ran nearly straight for it.

Smith passed him and took the point, following his compass. To the right was a rice paddy with a high dike around it. Smith avoided that, staying in the elephant grass. They were now so far from the camp that the grass was shoulder high on the Americans and above the heads of the Vietnamese.

Smith was breaking a path through it by stepping forward and twisting his foot. He had to be careful that he didn't make a lot of noise, but by breaking the path that way, he could move along ahead of the rest of the patrol and they would be able to follow him without actually needing to see him.

Breaking a trail through elephant grass was tiring, and Smith could only do it for about an hour. At another clump of trees, they halted for a brief rest. Then they moved off, staying inside the treeline for twenty meters, moved out, over a small graveyard holding only five graves in the strange built-up mounds and stone walls used in the wet delta area, and into another treeline.

In the trees, they slowed their rate, trying to move silently through the night. Around them they could hear animals scurrying, but nothing was bolting away from them.

At two, Kepler checked his compass and tried to

see the landmarks around him. Smith, having set up security, came back and said, "What's the problem?"

"Should have been there by now. I'm afraid we might have missed it."

"You sure we've gone far enough. I haven't seen any indication that we were even close to something."

Kepler pulled out his flashlight with the red lens cover on it. He unrolled his poncho, couched down so that he was sitting on the ground with the poncho covering his head. He checked to make sure that no light would leak and turned on the flashlight. He studied the map, saw a faint line that indicated an intermittent stream about two klicks west of the village. If they came to that, he would know for sure. There were no other obvious terrain features around. He would have to rely on his initial compass course.

He pulled the poncho off and said, "Let's take a twenty-minute break here. Drink some water. We should be okay."

At three, they still hadn't found the village of Cai Thoi, and Kepler was beginning to wonder if it hadn't been moved. Such an idea wasn't totally ridiculous, but even if the villagers had abandoned the site, the Green Berets would have found the empty hootches.

Kepler was getting worried because he couldn't understand how they could have missed it. He had figured the initial compass course from the clump of trees where they started after the barrage. He had checked the progress along the way, making sure that Smith and the other point men hadn't been misreading their compasses. Everything was right on. The only thing he could figure was that they weren't making the progress that they should have been.

He told Smith to take the point again and speed up. If they hadn't reached the village by four-thirty, they would stop, set up a perimeter, and wait for dark the next day. He wanted to be in place near Cai Thoi when the sun came up so they could observe the people.

Ten minutes later, Smith had stopped and, when Kepler caught up, said, "I think I hear something off to the left." He chuckled under his breath. "And from the smell, I think it's a water buffalo pen."

"Which direction?"

"Over there. Maybe fifty meters, maybe more."

"Let's check it out."

They moved off, with the patrol trailing behind them, providing rear security. They reached the edge of the trees and found a large clearing filled with hootches. On the far side, they could see one light, probably a lantern. Near the center of the village was a dying fire, and in its flickering light they could see the pole where the village chief's wife had been tied.

Kepler nodded to himself and then whispered to Smith. "Okay, this is it. Let's get set up. Check security and tell the strikers we'll be here for a couple of hours. Have them eat something, take a drink, and get some rest. Tomorrow we begin recruiting."

CHAPTER 3 _____

Gerber stood in the small building that was the control tower of the helicopter operations for the airfield. Bates had sent an NCO over to wake him up and then escort him back to the office. There, Bates had explained that he had called Special Forces headquarters in Nha Trang. The CO knew an aviation unit commander who was writing up a series of negative mission reports about working with the ARVN and was looking for something else to do. The two of them discussed it, went to the aviation unit's battalion, and then group headquarters, at both of which the plan was thought a good one.

With the aircraft in hand, so to speak, Bates went to talk with Brigadier General Billy Joe Crinshaw, who screamed that they couldn't go shifting helicopters around the countryside like so many checkers. At first, Crinshaw said he would do everything in his power to stop this insane idea. But then Bates said the one thing that made it right with Crinshaw.

43

"What difference does it make? They're not your airplanes."

Crinshaw sat back, rubbing the fine leather of his judge's chair, feeling the breeze stirred up by his brand-new, five-thousand-BTU air conditioner. "A good question. How about this? Go ahead with your plan, if no one else raises any objections, neither will I. Just make sure that your people take care of those aircraft."

By zero four hundred hours, the orders had been cut. In the aviation unit, wake-up had been scheduled for four-thirty, and the company commander posted a note in operations telling all flight crews to meet in the mess hall at five. He asked for volunteers to take five aircraft to a Green Beret camp for a couple of weeks. Nearly everyone volunteered because they didn't want to work with Marvin ARVN anymore.

A little after eight, a single HUEY landed near the tower. The crew chief jumped out the left side of the helicopter and ran across the grass to the waiting room under the tower. Inside he saw only one man, so he walked up and said, "Captain Gerber?"

"Yes."

"Come with me, sir. We'll head on out to your camp."

"You have the whole flight here?"

"No sir. Just the one ship. The others will follow later in the morning. They're going to be bringing a shitload of ammunition for us, some Cs, and the like. And two of them are going to be flying cover for the fuel trucks. We have two coming out of Saigon that should get to the camp about three or four."

Gerber looked around the room. It was fairly large,

had a wooden bar separating the waiting area from the operations room, a number of chairs, and a couple of tables. There was no one else inside.

"Should you be telling me all this in here?"

"Why not, sir. There's no one around. And besides, we'll have everything completed before Charlie hears about it." The crew chief looked around. "You have any gear."

Gerber held up the small satchel he carried. "Only this. And my rifle."

"The ship's waiting, sir."

Gerber was glad that he had taken a few minutes to call Karen Morrow and explain his sudden departure. She hadn't liked it, but took it in stride. It wasn't the first time it had happened.

Outside Cai Thoi, Kepler was asleep while Smith kept watch. Since their arrival, nothing had stirred, either in the village or in the trees surrounding it. Near dawn, people began moving around. At first there were a couple of women who came outside to start fires. One or two old men appeared and then some children. Smith leaned over and gently woke up Kepler.

It became lighter and one of the young women entered the center of the village, looking around furtively. Then she moved to the side of a hootch, pulled away a woven mat, and disappeared into a bunker. A moment later she reappeared, followed by three young men.

They were dressed only in khaki-colored shorts and sandals made of old tires. But they weren't acting like normal villagers. Rather than helping with the routine chores, they sat in front of the hootch and waited for someone to bring them something to eat.

"That could be our answer," whispered Kepler, but he didn't expand on what he meant.

Kepler waited a little longer, but no more military-age males appeared. When the little group had finished eating, they left the wooden bowls on the ground and went back to the hidden bunker. A few minutes later, they were outside again, holding black pajamas, rucksacks, and weapons.

Quickly, Kepler pointed to the left and then to the right. He had the strikers spread out. Kepler told Smith to work his way to the other side of the village as a one-man blocking force, but not to get so far away that they couldn't support him. He would have five minutes.

With one of the Vietnamese, Kepler moved to the south side of the village, using the hootches for cover. There, he worked his way around to the right, from one hootch to the next, aware that any moment someone might see him.

As he thought of that an old woman stepped out the door of the hootch in front of him, saw him and his weapon, and ducked back inside, pretending that she had seen nothing. Kepler didn't like leaving her behind him, but there wasn't much he could do, given the size of his patrol. Suddenly, the way things were breaking, he wished that he had opted for twenty men.

But apparently no one sounded an alarm. No one began a coughing attack or a sneezing spree. There was no warning system in the village. Kepler stepped right to the hootch where the young males were still putting on their clothes, their weapons leaning against the mud wall. In Vietnamese, he told them to put their hands up because they were his prisoners.

For a moment, time hung suspended as the three men wondered if they could get to their weapons. One of them started to slip to his right, trying to open the gap between them and Kepler, but Kepler wasn't going to fall for this. He fired once, the bullet smashing into the wall near the head of the man in the middle. His rifle barrel didn't waver, and each of the men knew that Kepler would shoot to kill next time. They froze.

The other villagers didn't react at all. They ignored what was happening, as if it had nothing to do with them. They had already seen what the VC would do. Now they waited to see what the Americans would do.

Kepler had one of the strikers with him pick up the enemy's weapons and unload them. Then, while he watched, each of the men was searched, and when this was finished, Kepler backed off. He whistled once and the rest of the patrol joined him. He told them to watch the males. Then he went off to ''arrest'' the young woman who had fed the VC. Finally, he searched for the chief's surviving daughter and ''arrested'' her too. That way, he figured no one would know she was the real target.

While two of the Vietnamese guarded the prisoners, Smith crawled into the hidden bunker. Although it was dark and he had somehow broken his light, he eventually located a small bundle of papers, a pistol, and three Chinese grenades. He pulled it all out after him. Then, almost as an afterthought, he tossed one of the grenades back in. An explosion a few seconds later collapsed part of the bunker.

Quickly, they searched the other hootches, finding nothing except a couple of rusty knives and the possessions of the villagers. Most sat staring in the distance as the Americans violated their homes. Kepler didn't like doing it, but felt he had to, to protect the cover he was building for the chief's daughter. They had to look like a normal patrol.

In the last hootch, under a worn bamboo mat, he found a rusting rifle. It was a single-shot weapon of French design that looked as if it belonged in the nineteenth century. At first, Kepler was going to take it, but he could find no ammo for it, and the barrel was in such bad shape that he feared it wouldn't fire without blowing up. He bowed to the old man in the hootch and handed the rifle back. The old man immediately hid it again.

Back in the center of Cai Thoi, Kepler saw that Smith had gotten everyone ready to move out. Before he left, Kepler stripped the little food that they had carried and left it piled in front of a cooking fire. Without a word, they filed out, toward the north.

As soon as they were out of sight of the village, they turned to the east, heading nearly straight back to the camp. The prisoners were in the center of the squad, watched by Smith. Kepler was in the rear, guarding their trail. One of the most trusted of the strikers was leading them. In less than two hours, they had arrived at the gate of Camp A-555.

The flight back to the camp didn't take long. As they approached, Gerber could see that four revetments had been finished and the fifth was under construction. The revetments weren't much, just two parallel lines of sandbags about four feet high. The helicopters were to be parked between them.

They landed on the north end of the runway, hovered to the right, and shut down. Gerber told the flight crew to hang loose there and he would send someone over to help them with their gear and show them to their quarters. He then ran off to the team house to see if there was a report from Kepler yet.

Kepler was sitting at a long table, sipping a cup of coffee. He had the papers taken that morning spread on the table in front of him, looking for anything of importance in them. At the top of the pile was the pistol Smith had found.

"Anything interesting?" asked Gerber.

"No sir. Can't really make anything out of this. I'll get it on the afternoon chopper to Saigon. I doubt seriously if there is anything here, but you can never tell."

"Maybe you better fill me in on this. I thought you were just after one person. What's all this?"

Kepler explained, ending by saying, "They don't know it, but the VC provided us with the perfect cover."

"So where's the girl?"

"Doc McMillan's looking at her. Some of the cuts looked a little bad so he's treating them and trying to get her cleaned up. I'm afraid that she's still pretty broken up over what happened."

"You expected something different?"

"No sir. Not really. I just thought that she would take it a little better than she has."

"She watched her family slaughtered. . . ."

"I know that, sir. It's not like this is something

that hasn't happened before, or that these people aren't aware of what is happening," he said coldly.

"Just take it easy on her. She's still basically just a kid."

The door opened and Lieutenant Bromhead came in. He sat down next to Gerber after pouring himself a cup of coffee. "Thought that was you coming in."

"We need to find space for the flight crews. Five of them. About twenty guys. And their gear," said Gerber.

"Kind of sudden, isn't it? We don't even know if the girl will cooperate."

"Well, Bates didn't let any grass grow under his feet if that's what you mean. I figured it would be a couple of days, but they woke me up this morning and told me that the ships would be arriving today. Thought we could throw up that general purpose tent we have. Might be a little crowded, but they're not going to be here all that long."

Kepler stood. "I better go over to the doc's and see how things are shaping up."

Gerber drained his cup and said, "Where's Fetterman?"

"Out with a patrol."

"Oh. Then find Tyme and send him over to the flight line."

"He's out with Fetterman."

Gerber turned to Bromhead. "Find someone to help the flight crews get settled and get a detail together to erect the tent. I'll be on the flight line."

At the northern end of the runway, Gerber found both pilots and took them aside. He introduced himself and then asked, "Has anyone told you what this is about?"

Ramsey, the aircraft commander, said, "No. They just asked for volunteers to work with the Special Forces. Since you guys are Americans and not ARVN, I jumped at it."

"We have three companies of Vietnamese strikers," said Gerber, wondering if he was saddled with a bigot.

"Yeah, but they're not ARVN. You have control over their training, and from everything I've heard, that training has been pretty good."

"We try," said Gerber.

"Besides," said Chrisman, the other pilot, "you won't have us flying around to pick up water bottles or landing a battalion in the field so they can have a picnic. The ARVN have had us do that. If we're going to be shot at, and maybe killed, we want it to be for something more than empty water bottles."

"I think, if things work out, that the mission will be somewhat more important than water bottles. It will help to finally secure this area."

Ramsey nodded. "I knew that coming down here wasn't a bad idea." He smiled. "Probably shouldn't say this, but there were more volunteers than there were slots. Everyone wanted to get away from Marvin ARVN."

Gerber then explained what they wanted to do. Ramsey nodded, listening, and when Gerber finished, Ramsey said, "We've done a couple of things like that, working with some American units. The key is to not get them so far out we can't reinforce or support them. Normally, with ten helicopters and other companies right near us, there is no problem, but you've got to remember that you only have five, and the closest support is about a twenty- to thirty-minute flight away."

"Well, all the details haven't been worked out. We expected to have a couple of days before you guys arrived. Since you're here, we'll have a strategy session later."

There were three loud pops and Gerber turned to the east, staring into the distance. To the flight crew he said, almost casually, "Incoming."

Ramsey was amazed for two reasons. One was that Gerber had announced the incoming so quickly, with hardly a clue, and two, that he stood there, looking into the east.

Gerber said, "There's the commo bunker across the strip. I'm going to the fire control tower."

"What about counter mortar?"

Gerber didn't answer. He was sprinting for the tower, cursing because it was the first time in a couple weeks that they had been hit during the day. He scrambled up the ladder and found Minh using binoculars to scan the rice paddies to the east.

"You see anything?"

The mortar rounds dropped far short, not even hitting the wire.

"Thought I caught a flash near that treeline."

Gerber picked up the extra binoculars. "Where?"

"Treeline about five hundred meters off to the north-northeast. Thought I caught one flash."

There were two more pops. Gerber turned to the south. "That sounded like it was near the river."

Both turned to look. The rounds dropped into the wire, blowing up some of the concertina. One of them set off a claymore mine.

"Didn't see that."

"Neither did I, old boy," said Minh, his British military training showing through in his thick Vietnamese accent.

When there was no more incoming, Gerber climbed down and walked back over to the helicopter. He noticed that the crew was still there, although the fronts of their fatigues were dusty, as if they had been lying down.

"What's this about counter mortar?"

"Simple. Each time we're hit, we scramble a couple of ships and look for the tubes. We can be over them in under two minutes," Ramsey explained. "It really inhibits them. It's quicker and more accurate than patrols and counter mortar artillery fire."

"You have a gunship coming?"

"No. But we do have door guns on these. And, if you give us a couple of guys, they can use M-14s out the door. VC mortar teams are usually only four or five guys without any heavy weapons, other than the tube."

"I don't know," said Gerber.

Chrisman chimed in. "It's a good idea, Captain. The only thing, we should take the guys up once or twice to get them used to firing out the doors. They have to be careful they don't shoot off the tail rotor or put rounds through the main rotor. And they have to learn how to track targets from a helicopter. Pete Browne, our door gunner, can give them some pointers."

Gerber said, "Once everyone gets here, we can go over some of these things. Right now, I need a recon flight."

"Why not combine the two. We can show some of

your guys what we mean and still do the recon. Kill two birds with one stone.''

"Okay. Okay." Gerber smiled. "I don't know if you guys are any good or not, but I like your enthusiasm. Let me talk to my exec and see when the patrol is due back. I have the perfect man for you. My light weapons specialist, Sergeant Tyme. He'll love the concept."

About noon Fetterman, Tyme, and twelve strikers entered the south gate. Gerber was there to greet them and to find out if they were too tired for a little airborne recon and training. Tyme was going to say no, that he had a lot to attend to, even if they had been in the field for only twenty-four hours, but then Gerber told him about the counter mortar.

"So you want a couple of us to go up and learn how to shoot out of a helicopter."

"That's right. Puts us on the target in less than a minute if we get the breaks."

"Just one question, Captain. Can I have an M-79 grenade launcher?"

"What for?"

"Isn't that obvious? A couple of guys firing machine guns at the target are good, but think of the confusion if I can drop a couple of M-79 rounds in their laps."

"Yeah." Gerber laughed. "You should take an M-79. Definitely you should take one."

It was early afternoon before they could get airborne. First, they had a cold lunch of C-rations. The flight crew didn't really care because they had had a hot breakfast and Gerber had promised a hot dinner.

Then Ramsey had wanted flight helmets for Tyme and Miles Clarke, one of the demolitions men. Unfortunately, the intercom in the back was set up for only two helmets, and Bocker, the commo man, spent nearly forty minutes adding the slots for two more jacks.

Finally, Ramsey took both Tyme and Clarke aside and said, "I know that both of you are professional soldiers, but this is something a little different than what you've experienced before. We use the solid metal mounts for the door guns because we don't want the gunners shooting up the cockpit or tail. Now, some of the new guys have been known to become so intense at following a target that they don't realize what they're doing. The stops on the gun protect the helicopter."

He smiled at the door gunner. "Pete here is so good, though, that we let him use a bungy cord if he wants. Listen to what he says because he's the professional at this."

"No problem, sir," said Tyme. "I'm just here to learn a new trade."

"Okay then, while Chrisman and I make a quick preflight, Pete can brief you."

Browne took Clarke and Tyme aside, showing them the M-60 machine guns and how they operated. He pointed out that the one on the left side had a case to catch the brass from the machine gun because it had a nasty habit of falling through the tail rotor. If the man on that side was using an M-14, he would have to be careful with the expended brass. The other thing was to make sure that the brass was ejected in such a way that it didn't hit the pilots or the other crewmen.

"Remember too that even if the target on the ground is stationary, we're moving, at about a hundred miles an hour. You have to lead your target or aim behind it to compensate. It's not really as hard as it sounds. If we start an orbit around the target, you have to adjust your aim accordingly."

He looked at the M-79 that Tyme had put into the cargo compartment. "I'm not real sure just what kind of problems you'll have with that. I guess we'll just have to experiment."

Ramsey climbed down from the rotor head as Gerber walked up. He unfolded a map and set it on the floor of the cargo compartment. When Ramsey moved to look at it, Gerber said, "Not really much to this. I'm just interested in seeing if there is unusual activity in this general area." He circled a small portion on the map near the Cambodian border. "You have to remember that Charlie has been alone here for years, and the only real setback he's suffered is our camp. You'll have to keep your eyes open."

"That shouldn't be a real problem, other than the proximity of the border. We don't want to violate that."

"I don't think there will be a problem with anyone filing complaints. Just how much can you see from the air?" asked Gerber.

"If we don't get any ground fire and are able to make our pass slow enough, we should be able to see any of the signs that you would. Oh, we won't see the broken blade of grass or bent twig, but if anything substantial, such as a squad-sized patrol, has been through there, we'll be able to tell."

Now Gerber shook his head. "I don't believe it. If I had to send a patrol out there, it would take two, three days. You're telling me I can have the information in a couple of hours."

"Don't sell the ground patrol short. Charlie can, if he wants, evade detection by us. Nothing really beats the man on the ground, but we can easily spot trends and tell you where your patrols will be the most advantageous."

The briefing complete, Ramsey climbed into the cockpit and strapped in. Chrisman did the same. When everyone was on board, Ramsey leaned across the pedestal, rolled on the throttle, pressed the flight idle detent button, and set the throttle on the low side. He then checked the switches one last time and said, "Clear."

Both the gunner and the crew chief looked to the sides and rear to make sure no one was standing under the tail rotor or behind the turbine. They responded with, "Clear right," and "Clear left."

Ramsey pulled the trigger and watched the engine temperature climb upward. When he saw it wasn't going to be a hot start, he rolled on the throttle and sat back in his seat.

With everything at operating speed, the radios on, and the gunners ready, Ramsey picked up to a hover, used the pedals to turn back toward the north, and took off. He climbed out slowly, watching the sky above him, while the door gunners watched the ground below. If there were any VC around, they ignored him and his helicopter.

They turned west, leveling off at fifteen hundred feet. That put them out of effective small arms range. At eighty knots, they were just cruising along. Over the intercom, Ramsey explained what he was doing for Tyme and Clarke.

In the area of the patrol, Ramsey told them to keep their eyes open. If they saw anything, they could fly lower, but they had to be careful. They could not use the same flight route twice because that gave Charlie time to set up, but if they used different routes, they could usually get away with it. And if they wanted a closer look, they could make a low-level pass.

It took only forty minutes to explore the whole patrol zone. They saw nothing of interest. That finished, they flew south to a swampy area that had been designated a free fire territory. It meant that no one should be in it so that they wouldn't hurt anyone if they fired all their weapons.

Ramsey found the wreckage of a South Vietnamese aircraft that had crashed a couple of months earlier. It would give them a target. While Browne explained the finer points of shooting from a moving gun platform, Ramsey flew a number of fast approaches at the wreckage. Both Tyme and Clarke fired at it. The tracers and splashes of water showed them where their rounds were going, allowing them to adjust their aim. It wasn't long before they both were riddling the tail section of the downed plane, firing their M-14s in short bursts.

Tyme then practiced with the M-79 until he was consistently dropping the rounds near the tail. Clarke tried a couple of shots but he didn't come very close.

As the last maneuver, Ramsey set up an orbit and let them practice that way. Both found it easier to hit the targets. Tyme used the last few rounds for the M-79 to practice from the orbit. He said that it was like dropping rocks into a barrel. It was too easy to believe.

They broke off the practice, headed for the nearest airfield to refuel and rearm, and then flew back to the camp. When they got there, they found that all the other flight crews had arrived, that the fuel trucks were there, and that a general briefing would be held right after dinner.

As Ramsey stepped out of the helicopter after shutting down, he said to Tyme, "I don't know about you, but I like this a lot better than working with the ARVN. You never know who they're going to shoot at. At least with you guys, we know which side you're on."

CHAPTER 4

While Tyme and Clarke were out learning how to shoot from helicopters, Gerber, Minh, Bromhead, and Lieutenant Bao, commander of the Tai strike company, were trying to decide who would be best on the reaction teams. They had to be trusted, good with weapons, and capable of fighting when they were outnumbered, because Gerber knew that the VC cadre they were after had a company of a hundred to a hundred and fifty men guarding it. At the most, the reaction team would have forty men. But they would have helicopter support and could call for TAC Air or limited artillery.

At first they were going to combine the strike force, using both Minh's South Vietnamese and Bao's Tai tribesmen. However, no one could be sure how the Vietnamese would react under Tai leadership or how the Tais would react under Vietnamese leadership. Finally two separate teams were set up, one commanded by Bao and one by Nuyen Cao Linh, a South

61

Vietnamese second lieutenant handpicked by Minh. When one was out, the other would be on standby in case there was trouble.

Training for the units, familiarizing them with the helicopters, giving them a couple of orientation flights, and teaching them how to get out of the helicopters would begin the next day. Gerber, realizing that Crinshaw and Bates wouldn't allow the helicopters to remain more than a couple of weeks, decided that training could only last one full day.

That finished, Gerber checked on the revetments that were being built to protect the fuel trucks and then went over to the team house. Fetterman, the diminutive team sergeant, was sitting at one of the tables, cleaning his silenced submachine gun. He had it broken down into nearly fifty pieces so that it resembled nothing at all.

Gerber sat down opposite him and asked, "How fast can you get it back together?"

"So that it will fire?" Fetterman grinned.

"Of course, so that it will fire."

"From this, four minutes and twenty seconds. I can field-strip and clean it in just under a minute. In the dark, it would take about two."

Gerber held up his hands. "Okay. Okay. I'm suitably impressed."

Fetterman put down his cleaning rod and looked Gerber in the eyes. "What is it, Captain?"

"Oh, nothing really. It's just this thing with the helicopters and the village chief's daughter. It's all moving too fast; no one has given us the time to think things all the way through."

"I'm afraid you've lost me, sir."

"Look at the fuel trucks. Never thought about

them. Hit one with a mortar and we'll have flaming JP-4 over two hundred square meters. The safest place to park them is outside the wire. Those revetments won't be much protection.''

"The odds that the VC will hit one of them are fairly low. More likely that they'll put a few holes in one so the fuel just leaks out.''

Gerber stood up, paced to the coffeepot and then back to the table. "I know that. I just don't like it. And we've now got two, three million dollars of extra equipment in camp. Not to mention an additional thirty Americans. We're no longer that little camp out in the boondocks. We're becoming the center of the war.''

"So, there's a problem?''

"No, not really. We'll be having the big meet tonight with the flight crews, probably just the pilots and one or two of the door gunners because of numbers. I want all the team to be there, though. Be thinking about this, and how we can best exploit it.''

"I always am, Captain.''

Gerber left then, realizing he hadn't explained his problem to Fetterman. Not that he really had one. It was just that he felt he was missing something vital, not because he was incompetent but because he didn't understand the tactics of the helicopters.

He had mentioned it to Fetterman because he respected Fetterman's judgment. Fetterman had been around since World War II and was used to having new weapons and tactics thrown at him. And he hadn't seemed all that concerned about everything.

But then, it wasn't Fetterman's problem. Gerber would just have to learn that all the Americans there, from the Special Forces soldiers to the flight crews, were professionals. He would have to trust them to do their jobs.

The meeting was little more than a rehash of everything else that had gone on before because no one really knew what they could do or how it would work. The pilots explained what they would need for landing zones, that an area big enough for the helicopter didn't necessarily mean that they could land in it, especially on a hot muggy day, or if there were tall trees around it.

Gerber tried to explain his needs and what they were really looking for. Naturally, any suspicious people should be checked, but the main thrust was to stop the VC propaganda cadre that was operating in the area.

Using a map, Gerber showed the flight crews where they suspected the VC hid, VC strongholds, and villages of VC. He pointed out that most of it didn't matter because the Cambodian border was so close that the VC could operate from there if they wanted too. In fact, he believed that the cadre they wanted was based in Cambodia and only ventured into Vietnam for short periods of time. "It's going to be hell to catch them."

They also talked about the counter mortar activity. One flight crew would remain with the aircraft each night. Tyme and Clarke would rush to them if there was incoming and they would try to get airborne in time to hit the enemy mortars.

Finally, Gerber covered up his map and said, "Seems that I'm missing something here. If anyone can think of what it is, I'd like to know."

No one said anything.

"Then I guess that's it. We'll just have to get into this thing and see how it goes."

The next morning, after the crew chiefs of each of the helicopters, using interpreters, explained to the strikers that everyone should be careful not to run into the tail rotor, the flight took off on its first mission. Still, there was no clear-cut assignment. Captain Larry Lucas, from the aviation detachment, took over the duties of command and control. Bromhead was in back of his helicopter, wearing a spare helmet. They were looking for a target while the rest of the flight, carrying a platoon of Bao's Tai tribesmen, were orbiting north of the camp.

Gerber, after seeing the flight off, accompanied Kepler over to the dispensary to see how the chief's daughter was. McMillan told them, "As we thought, the cuts were superficial. Very few of them did more than break the skin, although a couple of them were fairly deep. Used an antiseptic to clean them, after a good wash with soap and water. They all scabbed up pretty good and there isn't any sign of infection."

Kepler stood there listening and nodding and said, "But?"

"But. I'm afraid that the psychological damage may run deep. You can imagine what the terror must have been like. She had seen her mother beaten to death and her sister shot to death. There was no reason to suspect that the VC would not kill her also. She hasn't said much to me. Just a couple of Vietnamese phrases which basically are pleadings to be left alone. At least she doesn't jump every time I enter the room."

"Will she be able to function normally, doc?" asked Kepler.

"So that you can use her?"

Kepler shrugged. "Isn't it possible that helping us stop that VC cadre will help her recover?"

McMillan closed and locked the tiny drug cabinet. "I try to stay away from playing psychologist. There are too many variables, not to mention that the psychologists themselves don't know all the answers. Freud would have us believe that all this is somehow sexual. Jung would have another explanation, although he studied with Freud. Who knows? What you want might put her over the edge so that she can never recover, or she might see it as a way of committing suicide so that she will slip up the first chance she gets."

"Can I talk to her?"

McMillan shot Gerber a glance. Gerber nodded slightly, almost invisibly.

"Go easy with her. Very easy," said McMillan. "And I'll be in the room the whole time. I tell you to stop, you stop."

Kepler stepped toward the door, stopped, and turned. "I'm as interested in that girl's health as you are, but I've got my job to do too. You might not like it, but it has to be done."

"I know."

McMillan opened the door that led to a single room. It had been a storage area, but when they brought in the girl, McMillan had it cleaned. She was lying on a cot, flat on her back, staring at the ceiling. Gerber was amazed at how slight she looked. Her face was pale, surrounded by a mane of black hair. A camouflage poncho liner was pulled to her chin, and it looked almost as if there was no body in the bed, only a head, and the hair.

She didn't look at them when they entered. She either wasn't aware of them or was pretending that they weren't there.

McMillan stepped to the bed, took her hand out from under the cover, and checked her pulse. Not that he had to, but he thought that the touch of another human, someone who wanted nothing from her, might be comforting. She didn't react.

Kepler knelt on the floor beside her cot and asked, "Do we know her name?"

"No. You brought her in with the others. What did they say?"

"I didn't ask. I didn't want them to attach any significance to the fact that we picked her up. In fact, I had those people evacked out of here just as fast as possible. The ARVN have them in Saigon. They're supposed to get us something in a couple of days."

"Should you be discussing this in front of her?" asked Gerber. "I mean, we have no reason to suspect that she can't speak English."

Kepler reached out to touch her shoulder and said, "What's your name?"

She looked at McMillan, then at Kepler. Her eyes widened in fear as she saw the extra men in her room. She pulled away, almost in horror. She opened her mouth to scream but made no sound.

McMillan said softly, in Vietnamese, "It's all right. We're not going to hurt you."

But she seemed not to hear. She sat up and tried to scramble out of the bed. She closed her eyes. She balled both fists and pressed them into her mouth.

Kepler started to speak again, but McMillan cut him off and said, "Get out."

Kepler looked at Gerber.

"Let's go. Let the doc calm her down," the captain said.

"But . . ." protested Kepler.

"Let's just get out."

McMillan watched them go. Then he sat down on a rough wooden stool and began a slow monologue. He didn't really say much, switching from English to Vietnamese and back again. The girl opened her eyes and saw that the others were gone. She relaxed slightly.

McMillan got up and reached out for one of her hands. He took her fist, uncoiled the fingers of one hand. He pulled gently and she came toward him. He got her lying down and covered her again. Before he left, he said, "Don't worry, we won't let anyone hurt you." Then he translated it into Vietnamese.

In the outer room, McMillan found Kepler and Gerber. Before anyone could speak, Gerber said, "How old is she?"

"Who knows?" asked McMillan. "She could be fifteen or thirty-five. It's hard to tell. I opt for the lower end of the scale, maybe seventeen or eighteen."

"When can we talk to her?"

"Maybe you shouldn't. You saw how she acted."

Kepler turned to Gerber. "Captain, you can't let him do this. We already discussed this and you agreed to it. She'll make the perfect agent."

"Not if you can't even get her to talk to you," interrupted McMillan.

Gerber said, "Look, I've never been sold on this

network of agents you're building. We're supposed to be soldiers, not the goddamned CIA.''

"Captain, solid military intelligence can win battles and save lives. We won at Midway because we knew the Japanese would be there.''

"I don't want to argue about it. And I'm not going to interfere in your operation; I'm merely commenting on a fact. But I do want you to go easy on this one. She may be of no value to us anyway, but if we force her over the edge, she'll definitely be of no value.''

On the ground, two thousand feet below them, Lieutenant Bromhead thought that he saw a group of men scatter for a lone clump of trees. He pressed the button for the intercom and said, ''I've got movement.''

Lucas broke around to the right and orbited the trees once but didn't see anything. He turned north, descended to a thousand feet, and crossed over the top of the trees. Still, he didn't see anything, so he descended again and approached from a different direction. Before he got close to the trees, there was a burst of automatic weapons fire. Lucas jerked in pitch and broke to the left.

On the intercom, he said, ''Looks like we found them.''

Bromhead said, ''What do we do now?''

"How many did you see?''

"Seven or eight, but I didn't see any weapons.'' He laughed. ''But I guess we can assume they have some.''

Lucas got on the radio to flight head. ''Vampire one-one, this is Vampire one-six.''

"Go one-six."

"Turn northeast. We're orbiting about four klicks north of point Tango X-ray. Call when you have us in sight."

Three minutes later, Vampire one-one called. "We have you in sight."

"Roger. Target area is stand of trees to your eleven o'clock. Do you have it in sight?"

"East side has three rice paddies in a line with one hootch at the far side."

"That's it. There are eight, maybe ten VC in the trees and we have taken fire. Suggest you have three ships approach the east side, touch down near the hootch. Break trail off and have him land on north side of the trees, landing about a hundred meters away near that small stream."

"Roger, one-six. Will we have gun support?"

"Negative. You have full suppression on the trees. Make your approach from south to north. When you're ready."

"We are rolling over. Trail, call your break."

"We'll be breaking now," said the trail pilot.

No one, not in the C and C, lead, or even Bromhead, realized that by breaking trail off, they were putting the two Americans down with five Tai tribesmen in one location and Bao and the rest in another. Bao would have to organize the assault on the treeline without help from either Fetterman or Bocker.

Trail broke down and to the left, circling the treeline at fifty feet and nearly a hundred knots. A single burst of AK fire was directed at them, and the door gunner responded with his M-60 machine gun. They passed the western edge, and then, in front of them, the pilot saw a small stream. He raced toward it, flared, and kicked the pedals as he pulled pitch. With the rotors now clawing at the air perpendicular to the ground, they slowed abruptly, forcing everyone down in their seats. As the helicopter began to drop to its side, the pilot leveled the skids so that he could touch down.

Two or three automatic weapons in the trees opened fire, but most of the bullets missed the helicopter. One or two struck the tail boom. The door gunner, seeing the flashes and watching the enemy's tracers, returned the fire. He didn't see anything more but hoped to keep the heads of the enemy down.

Over the intercom, the crew chief said, "We're unloaded."

"Roger." The pilot keyed the mike of the radio and said, "Trail's on the go."

The three-helicopter flight descended slowly toward a touchdown near the lone hootch. Ramsey used the radio. "Flight, fire when ready."

The crew chiefs all opened up, hitting the trees nearest to them. The door gunners, facing open rice paddies, held their fire, looking for a target. An enemy on that side of the flight would have to expose himself completely if he wanted to shoot.

The flight touched down about twenty meters from the hootch. Just as lead's skids hit the dirt, two trapdoors in the roof of the hootch popped up and snipers began taking potshots at them. Ramsey's windshield disintegrated in an explosion of plexiglass. The instrument panel fell apart as bullets slammed into it.

Bao and his men jumped out the other side of the

aircraft and scrambled for cover behind the tiny rice paddy dikes. They had their weapons ready but didn't fire because the helicopters were between them and the enemy. It was an amazing display of self-discipline for Tais.

The crew chief in lead almost stepped out of the aircraft in his attempt to return fire. The tracers from his M-60 set the thatch of the roof ablaze, and his rounds tore through it, killing one of the Viet Cong and wounding the other. The shooting from there ended.

With the troops out, lead pulled pitch, rolled over, and in a nose-low attitude, climbed out, gaining speed. In seconds, after taking a few rounds from the trees, they were out of the area and safe overhead, orbiting.

Bao and his most trusted, as well as his most bloodthirsty sergeant, Krung, stayed behind the dike. The others popped up periodically, firing at the trees, but all were unsure of what they should do. They thought they should attack the trees, but each time they stood up, the volume of incoming fire increased so much that they couldn't move. They were stuck.

In C and C, Lucas said, over the intercom, "Why don't they move?"

Bromhead looked down, saw Bao and his men firing into the trees but not moving toward them. He said, "They've been trained for defense. We've taught them how to establish fields of fire, how to pick targets, and to put out rounds. We haven't had the time to teach them how to assault an enemy position."

"What are we going to do?"

"First," said Bromhead, "we're going to have to make sure that when we divide a flight, we have some of our people in each group. Shouldn't have put both Fetterman and Bocker on one ship.''

"That's great, Lieutenant, but doesn't answer the question.''

"Right. We'll have to land so that I can direct Bao and his troops. Is that possible?''

"Sure. When?''

"In a minute.'' Bromhead switched his control from intercom to radio. "Zulu seven, this is Zulu five.''

On the ground, Fetterman pulled the PRC-10 closer and keyed his mike. "Go, five.''

"Situation?''

"Some incoming fire, which we're returning. No big thing. We've dispersed so that we can cover the November and the whiskey sides of the trees.''

"Roger.'' Bromhead switched back to the intercom. "Okay, I need to go down now. Once I'm out, you might want to send the ships back to pick up the reserves, just in case. Tell them that we'll be more interested in ammo and possibly a couple of M-79s.''

"Roger. Can't you use the radio to direct the operation?''

"Could, but it will be better if I'm on the ground. If the troops see one of us with them, they feel better about it.''

Bromhead used the radio to alert Gerber at the camp that he would be on the ground, and the link between them would have to be Lucas relaying everything. Gerber wasn't happy about it, but he didn't say anything because Bromhead was the man on the scene. It was one of those problems that developed because no one had done this before.

When he finished the radio calls, Bromhead told Lucas that it was time. Lucas broke the orbit, dived for the ground, and then circled the area. He approached from the east, heading straight for the hootch instead of coming at it from the south as the flight had done. He flared, sucked in pitch, and dropped to the rice paddies behind Bao and his men. Bromhead dived out of the aircraft, and almost before he hit the ground, Lucas was on the go. He made a pedal turn and shot into the sky, taking no fire at all.

Bromhead leaped the dike and, in a crouch, sprinted across the open ground. He flopped down beside Bao.

Bao smiled and said, "Hi, Lieutenant Johnny. We not able to do much."

"We'll change that now." Bromhead looked over the dike, saw a couple of flashes from the VC weapons. But the fire wasn't concentrated. It was as if they were shooting just to let Bromhead know that they were around.

With his own rifle, Bromhead fired a couple of rounds into the trees, hoping that the enemy would shoot back. Two automatic weapons opened fire, one of them a light machine gun. Bromhead saw the muzzle flashes, locating the weapons.

"Get the guys with the M-79s up here. You should have three of them."

Bao turned to Krung and told him. Krung crawled off, keeping down and resenting the fact that he couldn't see any of the Viet Cong so he could kill them. But he had already learned that if he listened to the Green Berets, he would have a chance to kill lots of VC. And Krung had only one pleasure in life: killing lots of VC.

Once the three men were there, Bromhead pointed out the targets. Then he said, "When I tell you, I want you to start firing the HE rounds into the trees as fast as you can. Keep them going. But be careful because we'll be moving in behind them. When we get close, you stop."

They all nodded their understanding.

To Bao, he said, "When they start that, we'll move forward. I want three guys to take the hootch. Check for papers, weapons, and hidden bunkers. There may be a tunnel from it into the trees, and if there is, I want those guys to cover it. They are to secure that hootch and stay there. Understand?"

"Of course, Lieutenant Johnny."

"If they don't, then the VC might get behind us."

"I send my best corporal."

"Good. Now the rest of us will run to the trees. We want to keep our heads down and our weapons level, shooting forward as we move. We must be careful not to shoot each other. Once we reach the trees, we will take cover and scope out the situation."

Bao and Krung translated what Bromhead had said, even though everyone on the assault force understood some English. While they were doing so, Bromhead used the PRC-10 to tell Fetterman and Bocker that he was moving into the trees.

"Roger that, Zulu five. We will hold our fire."

When everything was set, the Tais, crouching behind the dikes and ready to run, their weapons held up, Bromhead nodded. The first three rounds from the M-79s arced toward the trees. One fell short, exploded in a cloud of black smoke and red dirt. The other two hit trees.

They were immediately answered by machine-gun and small arms fire. More grenades were fired rapidly and the enemy shooting began to die. When Bromhead noticed this, he yelled, "Let's go," and leaped to his feet.

Around him, the Tais did the same. They ran forward, some firing as they went. The three designated for the hootch broke that way. One of them slammed into the mud wall near the door and tossed a grenade in. After it exploded they dived in, being careful to miss the smoldering remains of the thatch roof. They found the body of one dead VC. His weapon was gone.

Bromhead reached the trees and hit the ground. In front of him, he saw an enemy soldier break cover to run backward. Bromhead dropped him with a single shot.

The grenadiers stopped shooting. When they did, Bromhead got to his feet and entered the treeline. He saw the body of a Viet Cong and ran to it, kicking the weapon away from his outstretched hand. He bent and took the magazine out of it, but he didn't move the body, afraid that the VC might have boobytrapped it.

Krung entered the trees and didn't stop. He ran toward the machine-gun position, which had begun firing again. He came on it from the left and leaped among the enemy soldiers there. The machine gunner kept shooting, ignoring him. Krung threw away his rifle and pulled his K-bar. He slit the throat of the assistant gunner and turned, driving his knife into the chest of the ammunition bearer. Then he jumped on the back of the machine gunner, pulled his head up and back, and cut his throat.

Another of the Tai tribesmen ran past Krung, who was now hacking off the genitals of the enemy dead to add to his trophy collection. The Tai ran toward a large bush. A burst of AK fire caught him in the chest and dropped him. He was dead before he hit the ground.

From behind Krung, another Tai opened fire and wounded the VC hidden in the bush. He ran forward then, and saw the VC try to pick up his weapon. The Tai fired again and the enemy's head exploded.

At that point, a dozen VC broke from cover, fleeing toward the rear, away from the assaulting Tais. One or two turned to fire wildly but that didn't stop the Tais. They shot back. Two more of the Viet Cong fell.

Finally the VC ran out of the treeline, trying to escape but running instead into a wall of fire thrown up by Fetterman and Bocker. They wouldn't allow the Tais with them to fire because of the danger of hitting Bromhead and his group, who were still in the trees. But Fetterman and Bocker were picking their targets. They killed four and wounded three more before the enemy VC threw down their weapons yelling, "Chieu hoi. Chieu hoi."

Bromhead came out of the trees behind the VC. He, Bao, and Krung advanced slowly, keeping them covered. Bromhead kept one eye on Krung, afraid that the Tai would allow his hatred of the Viet Cong to overwhelm him. But Krung didn't shoot.

They took the weapons from the enemy and pushed the VC toward Fetterman. Fetterman took charge of them, had them kneel while Bocker covered them. To Bromhead he said, "What now?"

"Sweep back through the trees to see if we missed anything, search for weapons, and check the bodies."

Bromhead organized the men quickly and started the sweep. They checked under the bushes, behind trees, and prodded the ground, looking for spider holes. They found nine bodies. One of them had a pistol, which Bromhead took for the moment. They found a packet of papers on this body. They also found a number of wallets containing pictures, ID cards, and money. Bromhead took all of it and wrapped it in a large handkerchief. He would turn it over to Kepler for any intelligence value it might have.

At the edge of the trees, they found two dead Tais. Three had been wounded and they were in the open, near the hootch. Bromhead walked into the hootch. There was nothing in there other than the one body. But the Tais had found a tunnel entrance. None of them wanted to enter.

Bromhead got close to it and tossed a grenade down. There was a muffled explosion and smoke boiled out of the opening. Bromhead asked Bao if he wanted to explore it.

"I not do it, Lieutenant Johnny. VC crawl in ground, not Tai."

"Okay. You guys keep me covered." Bromhead dropped into the hole and crawled forward. There was very little light and he waited for a moment, letting his eyes adjust.

About ten feet into it, he found another body. He grabbed one arm and dragged it back, pushing up and out. He reentered and found his way blocked. The grenade had caused part of the tunnel to collapse.

Bromhead got back out. He looked at the hootch, wished that they had the explosives to blow it up, but they didn't. So he gathered everyone together, had them pick up everything, including the enemy body, and left.

Outside, he saw that Fetterman and Bocker had brought the prisoners around. Bromhead told them to set up a perimeter for security. He then called for the helicopters. Lucas told him that he would have to wait while they dropped off the reserves. Bromhead had Lucas land so that he could evac the wounded to Doc McMillan.

Not long after this, the choppers returned, picked up everyone, and headed back to the camp. They landed to let off troops. They then headed to Saigon to refuel and rearm again, not wanting to tap the limited fuel supplies at camp unnecessarily. Ramsey flew back to the base at Bien Hoa to get a replacement aircraft. The one he had was too full of holes to be repaired at the Special Forces camp.

CHAPTER 5 _____

Kepler was on the runway when the flight landed. He had brought a group of Tais to serve as guards for the prisoners. As soon as they were off the aircraft, he separated them and sent them to different locations. He wanted to make sure that none of them exchanged information or knew what the others had said. He also thought that a lone man might be more inclined to talk than a group, whose members could draw on each other for support.

The youngest of the prisoners was taken to the team house. Kepler waited outside for a few minutes. The Tais made the prisoner stand and stared at him, as if daring him to make a move, but they didn't touch him. It was a not too subtle variation of the good cop–bad cop routine.

Kepler walked into the room, pulled a chair out from under the table, and sat down facing the prisoner. For a moment he sat there, and then said, "Do you speak English?"

The man didn't say a word. He stared at Kepler, the fear unmistakable in his eyes.

In Vietnamese, Kepler said, "Do you speak English?"

This time there was a reaction, as if the prisoner hadn't expected an American to be able to speak his language. But he still didn't say anything.

Kepler offered him a chair and told him to relax, that he wasn't going to be hurt. Kepler asked for his name.

Still the man refused to speak.

"You can tell me your name. And your rank. Neither of those is military information. It will help make things easier for you."

"Phan Dinh Thanh."

"Very good." Kepler nodded. "You know, we tell our soldiers that they can give their names, ranks, service numbers, and dates of birth. None of those help the enemy but might provide the captor with information that will make life easier for everyone."

Thanh stood still.

"So, how old are you, Phan?" When there was no answer, Kepler said, "That information can't hurt your fellows. I mean, we know that you're not going to tell me where your base is or how many men are there. We don't care about that anyway, because it's in Cambodia and we can't go there."

This surprised Thanh. First because the American seemed so sure that his base was in Cambodia, and then because he told him that the Americans couldn't go to Cambodia. He had been warned that the Americans, if they caught him, would beat him and torture him. He hadn't been told that they would sit in a room and calmly discuss things.

In fact, nothing had been exactly like he had been told. He hadn't wanted to surrender with the others because he was sure that they would be executed. The airlift to the camp was nearly torture because he expected to be thrown out the doors at any moment. No one had touched him, other than to make sure that he carried no weapons and to take his wallet.

The wallet wasn't much. It had been cheap and held only his ID card, a little money, and a picture of his sisters.

Kepler pulled the wallet out of his pocket and handed it back. "I think this is yours. You have to remember that we are not thieves or murderers. We are here to assist our friends." Again Kepler pointed to the chair. "Why don't you sit down? Would you like something to drink?"

Without thinking, Thanh sat down, going through his wallet. He was surprised to see that his money was still there, not realizing that North Vietnamese Dongs wouldn't be much good in South Vietnam, except as souvenirs. He looked up at Kepler but didn't say a word.

"I understand how you feel." Kepler smiled. "Alone in a foreign country. I mean, it's the same for me. Maybe a little harder because I come from a different culture. But you're wondering what's going to happen to you now."

Kepler got up, found a glass, and poured some water for Thanh. "Well, we're just going to send you to Saigon where you'll be in a camp with others who have been captured. Since you're young, you'll probably be sent home as soon as some kind of prisoner exchange can be arranged."

Right on cue, Lieutenant Minh burst into the room.

He grabbed the prisoner and jerked him to his feet. He screamed at Kepler, "What are you doing? We should kill this stinking pile of filth. He is not worth the time it would take to kill him."

Kepler pushed Minh out of the way. "Get out of here, Lieutenant. He's doing the best he can."

Leaning past Kepler, Minh swung at the prisoner, hitting him on the shoulder. "You just leave. I will take care of him."

Now Kepler moved, ignoring Thanh. He grabbed Minh and pushed him out the door. As he did, he winked once to tell Minh that the performance had been great.

"Please," said Kepler to the trembling Thanh. "Sit down and we'll talk."

All of this confused Thanh. He wasn't ready for the Americans to protect him. He didn't know what to do. This was not the brutal interrogation that he had expected.

"Well," said Kepler, "you never told me how old you are."

"Nineteen." Thanh couldn't see how that would hurt anything.

"Nineteen, huh? Been away from home long?"

"No. Only a few months," said Thanh cautiously.

"I've only been here a couple of months myself. Of course, I've been away from home longer than that. You like the camp in Cambodia?"

Thanh couldn't see where his personal opinion about the camp would be divulging military information. He said, "It's all right. We even have electricity."

"So do we." Kepler pointed to a single bare light bulb overhead. "Say, I'll bet you haven't had much training yet. Takes a long time to train a soldier in the United States. But you guys have one fellow who seems to be top-notch.''

Again Thanh was surprised. Now the big American was complimenting his comrades. He said, somewhat offhandedly, ''Yes, we have a Chinese adviser who helps us.''

''Oh, sort of like us helping the South Vietnamese,'' said Kepler evenly. It was obvious that the kid didn't know what he had just disclosed. ''Does he lead the group?''

''One of them. He tries to help the others too. So that we can throw the imperialistic aggressors out of our homeland.'' Thanh looked startled at what he had just said.

Kepler laughed. ''We hear the same thing, except we hear about the invaders from the north.'' He wanted to find a way to ask about the propaganda cadre, believing that Thanh might know something about it. His unit could be the one providing cover for the cadre.

He couldn't think of anything clever, so he just blurted it out. ''Say, you have anything to do with that special squad working around here?''

''They stay by themselves. They left yesterday for Tuy Dong.''

This had been the thing he wanted. To keep Thanh off balance, he said, ''Listen, you've been in the field for a while. You're probably hungry. Let me get you a sandwich.''

''Do I really have to go to Saigon?''

''Why not? What's wrong with that?''

Thanh didn't speak.

''We don't have the facilities for POWs here. The

rest of your friends will be sent out tonight. You'll be alone here.''

"I would prefer it here."

Kepler walked to the back of the room and made a sandwich, thinking that it wasn't a very Vietnamese meal, but then figured that it didn't matter. He gave the food to Thanh and told the Tais to keep him there but not to touch him.

Gerber was in the commo bunker making a report to Saigon about the mission that morning, trying not to say too much because anyone could be listening. Bromhead was with him, a map of the local AO spread out, grease pencil marks all over it, detailing the assault on the treeline.

Kepler entered and stopped. He looked at Bromhead, surprised once again by the young lieutenant. He had originally expected Bromhead to be a problem because of his age and lack of real experience, but the assault that morning had showed that Bromhead was very good at small unit tactics.

"Say, Johnny," said Kepler, "any chance that we can keep one of the prisoners?"

"Whatever for?"

"Well, that young guy you picked up hasn't learned much about military operations, but he's seen enough to give us some good stuff."

Gerber tossed the microphone to Bocker and said, "I don't think I ever want to talk to those jerks again. You better get together with Fetterman and get something on paper that we can send in tomorrow.''

"Right sir." Bocker left to look for Fetterman, leaving only his Vietnamese counterpart on watch.

Gerber stepped over to Kepler and said, "Now, what did you say?"

"I was telling Johnny that I would like to keep the one prisoner here for further interrogation. He's already dropped a couple of gems on me and I've only talked to him for an hour."

"Such as?"

"First, that guy who gave us fits on that operation on the border, the one who organized the troops and got them going when everyone else was running around in circles. You know the one?"

"I remember," said Gerber. "Might have been the same one who nearly broke up your ambush."

"Yeah," said Kepler. "I think it's the same guy now. Kid told me they have a Chinese adviser. We joked about his role being a lot like ours."

"Okay," said Gerber, impressed. "That's one."

"He also told me that the propaganda cadre will be working near Tuy Dong. Left yesterday."

Gerber moved straight to the map, looked at it, and flipped it over, finding the tiny village hidden deep in the swamps southwest of the camp. "Not that far away."

"Yeah," said Kepler. "I thought you'd appreciate that."

Gerber looked at Bromhead, who said, "You know how hard it is to get intelligence out of Saigon. A lot of stuff goes in but nothing comes out. It's like they want to push pins in their maps but won't give us anything so we can push pins."

"I think we can find something more impressive to do with it than stick pins in maps," said Gerber sourly.

"You know what I mean."

To Kepler, he said, "What do you plan to do with this prisoner. We don't have a compound for him. Krung and his bunch aren't going to be real pleased with a live VC in the camp."

"I thought that we could maybe build a one-room hootch over near the fuel trucks and put a couple of strands of barbed wire around it. We have plenty of people for a guard. One guy watches every four hours."

"I don't like it much," said Gerber.

"That's what you say about everything I try to do." It sounded like a complaint, but Kepler's voice made it a simple statement of fact.

"How long do you want to keep him here?"

"A couple of weeks. Then maybe we could release him."

"Are you out of your mind?" asked Bromhead. "Bring him into camp, let him stay for a couple of weeks and then send him back? He'd tell everything he knew."

Kepler smiled almost as if Bromhead had walked into a trap. "That's what I'm counting on. He would go back, without a whole lot of useful military information, but telling about humane treatment. Could make things a little easier. Instead of holding out until we assault them, some of them might be more inclined to surrender."

"That's expecting a lot," said Gerber. "I doubt that he would change many minds."

"Doesn't really matter, Captain. It might help, someday. But you know what those Vietnamese in Saigon will do to him. He's just a kid with almost no training."

Gerber was quiet for a minute and then said, "Here's

what we'll do. Send the others into Saigon tonight, just as soon as we can get a ship out here to pick them up. Lock your prisoner in the storage room, the one holding the paint, but have someone keep an eye on him. We'll check out some of that information, and if it proves to be good, we'll try to hang on to him.''

''And when we're through?''

''If I turn him loose, Crinshaw will hit the fucking roof. And I do mean hit it.''

''So?'' asked Kepler.

''So, we'll see.''

At seventeen hundred hours, Gerber was again meeting with his team and the pilots. He was standing in front of a map that outlined the mission flown that morning. Although it wasn't a real debriefing, it was the next thing to it.

''Most of you know what happened this morning. I think we should commend Lieutenant Bromhead for his handling of the assault. He did an excellent job. In case you haven't heard, we had two killed and three wounded. The VC lost fifteen dead and four captured, not to mention the weapons and documents found.''

Gerber nodded and Bromhead opened the rear door. ''Gentlemen, this is Lieutenant Bao, the commander of the Tai detachment we have here.'' Gerber waved Bao to the front and said, ''I think Lieutenant Johnny has something to say.''

''I sure do,'' said Bromhead, coming forward. ''You did one hell of a job this morning. You—''

''I did nothing, Lieutenant Johnny,'' protested Bao.

''You did. Sure, I had to help direct the assault,

but that was only because we hadn't shown you how to do it. You and your men did all the work.''

Bao nodded gravely.

''And because of that, we''—Bromhead waved a hand to indicate everyone, although he was referring only to the Special Forces men—''all of us, wanted you to have this.'' Bromhead held out the pistol that they had taken off the dead Viet Cong officer. ''You and your men earned it.''

Slowly Bao reached out. A dark hand touched the pistol, almost as if afraid of it. ''This is for men, Lieutenant Johnny.''

''Of course. For doing such a fine job.''

The others in the room began to applaud and Bao was hard pressed to keep from showing how touched he was. He accepted the pistol lovingly and then held it above his head so that all in the room could see it.

''A fine job,'' yelled Fetterman.

With the presentation out of the way and Bao heading back to show his men their trophy, Gerber took over again. ''I think that it might be helpful to talk about the mission.''

Bromhead jumped right in. ''The first thing we learned was that we need to split our men up so that we don't have them all on the same ship. That was the reason that I had to land.

''And we learned that a four-ship assault is fine against a small enemy force, but if we run into anything too large, we're going to be in trouble.''

''You can always call for air support or artillery,'' Gerber reminded him.

''Of course, if they are available. But today we weren't under an artillery umbrella. And you know how long it takes to get any air support out of Saigon unless you've already got it laid on. Then if we don't find them a mission, they go away mad and won't help us the next time."

Gerber turned to Lucas. "Your people have anything they want to say while we're critiquing this."

"We should have some kind of gunship support on these LZs. Door guns are nice, but nothing beats an armed ship."

"Can't deliver that. Crinshaw caused enough trouble with sending the slicks. If we know that an LZ is hot, we might be able to get something but it would take an hour. That would give the enemy time to slip away. Besides, tonight we really should try to find that propaganda cadre. Once that is done, you guys go home."

Lucas stood up, shaking his hands. "Wait a minute here. You said tonight?"

"Any other old business? Johnny?"

"Only thing I want to say to the flight crews is that I thought they did a hell of a job too. We've got quite a store of captured weapons, and if any of you, crew chiefs and gunners included, would like a souvenir, feel free to ask."

"I'll second that," said Gerber.

"That's very generous," said Lucas.

"Not at all. We've got so many of them that we're only too happy to share them."

"If there is nothing else . . ." said Gerber. "No?" He looked to Bromhead and Fetterman. "We'll want to work out some tactics later on. Right now," he said to the whole group, "we need to talk about a possible night mission."

He turned to pull the cloth off the second map, but a loud crump outside stopped him.

"Incoming!"

Fetterman yelled, "Counter mortar!"

Tyme and Clarke pushed themselves off the floor and ran for the door. Ramsey and Chrisman did the same, following the two NCOs. Ramsey hollered at them, "You grab your gear and we'll get the helicopter cranked."

At the aircraft, they found the crew chief had already untied the blade and removed the covers on the air filters. Both door guns were mounted and both pilots' doors were open.

"Well done," said Ramsey as he jumped into the cockpit.

Chrisman rolled the throttle to flight idle detent, looked out the door, and shouted, "Clear." He pulled the trigger, beginning the start sequence.

Two more mortars hit the camp, one near the fire control tower and one near the south wall.

Out of the dark, Tyme and Clarke sprinted. They ducked their heads and leaped into the cargo compartment. Two spare helmets were already sitting out. Tyme picked one up and put it on. Over the intercom he said. "We're ready."

Almost before the words were out of his mouth, the helicopter leaped into the sky, climbing rapidly. Ramsey said, "Someone said the mortars were to the east." He turned in that direction.

Tyme crouched between the pilots' seats so that he could look out the windshield. He picked up one flash and slapped Ramsey on the shoulder. "There. Over there. You see it?"

Ramsey nodded. "Got it. Everyone ready. We're going in."

The aircraft banked and dived. Both door guns opened fire forward. Tracers looped out, bouncing across the ground near the spot where the mortar flash had been.

Seconds later, the green tracers used by the VC began lacing the sky around them. Tyme laughed over the intercom. "The dummies are showing us where they are." He braced himself against one side of the cargo compartment door and fired the M-79. Beneath them, he saw the explosion, a shower of white sparks.

More tracers came at them. Clarke sat on the other side of the door, near the crew chief, firing his M-14 nearly as fast as he could change the magazines. The crew chief was using his M-60 machine gun. Red tracers going down. Green coming up.

"We're taking hits," said Ramsey.

Tyme ignored him, feeding rounds through the M-79. He switched from HE to WP—from high explosive to white phosphorus. The latter exploded in flashes of fire, lighting the ground. Suddenly, they could see men running below. A couple fell and the ground fire suddenly ceased as the enemy realized that they had been found. Now they were trying to find cover before they were killed. Their mortar tube had been destroyed by Tyme's first shot. He didn't know it. It was one of those lucky breaks.

Ramsey broke the orbit, turned and flew toward the south. Then, at low level, he approached the fires again at high speed. If there were any Viet Cong down there who wanted to shoot, he wanted to give them a fast-moving target. Either he was successful, or the VC had all run away. After ten minutes of fruitless searching, he headed back for the camp.

On the way, Chrisman switched the control heads on the intercom system to "Private" so that he could talk to Ramsey without any of the others listening.

"Do you know how far out our asses were hanging back there?"

"Don't sweat it, Fred. We were fine."

"Fine? The gunships don't even attack in single ship. What would have happened if we had been shot down?"

"From a thousand feet, I would have autorotated back toward the camp. They could have had people out to us in less than five minutes."

As the junior pilot, Chrisman couldn't say a whole lot. He had voiced his opinion. He shrugged and switched the intercoms back. He would talk to Lucas if he had the chance.

"I don't suppose we could land to look things over," said Tyme.

"Not a good idea. We would be an easy target. Our only advantages are speed and maneuverability. On the ground we're just a big fat pile of metal waiting to blow up."

At camp, they shut down. The door gunner ran off looking for the fuel truck driver so that he could top off the tanks. The crew chief was using a flashlight to check for damage to the helicopter, but all he could find was a couple of bullet holes in the metal skin of the tail boom and one round that went through the top of the cargo compartment. They lucked out because it hadn't gone through a rotorblade.

Ramsey went off to report to Lucas, and once they had done so, they all went back to the meeting that had been interrupted earlier.

* * *

Gerber was standing in front of his map. He pointed to a small village in the swampy area. "We have reason to believe that the VC cadre will be here tonight for one of their political speeches. Given the distance and the terrain, there is no way that we could get a patrol in there in time. We can, however, put the flight in.

"The only problem is that we know that the cadre is guarded by an infantry company. That means that we'll be outnumbered about two to one, or three to one. In a standup fight, I don't think we could win.

"But, if we can put a force on the ground and sweep through there quickly and then retreat, we could disrupt the meeting, and at this stage, it might be enough."

Gerber then outlined his plan. Put forty men on the ground just south of the village, have them basically run through it, shooting as many of the enemy as they could, and evacuate to the north where the helicopters would be waiting. They would leap on the choppers and depart the area.

"We won't be getting a body count so Saigon won't be able to see any benefit from the mission. The results will be measured by the number of men we get out of it unharmed and by the disruption to the meeting. No longer will the VC be able to claim they are invulnerable. They come out for a meeting, and we show up. Sure, we don't hang around. But we are there. It should be bad for their morale as well as their image. That's all we'll want for now."

"Just how are we supposed to find this village at night?"

"Shouldn't be too hard," said Kepler from the

back. "If they follow the standard procedure, they will build a big fire in the center of it to light the proceedings. It will be the only point of light out there."

Lucas said, "It sounds like a good plan, except that we'll be landing in the dark. We'll have to use landing lights and that will show the enemy right where we are. If we come down too close to the VC, I'm afraid you might lose five helicopters."

"How long do you have to leave the lights on?"

"With the weather the way it is and the moon, we can see fairly well. Only have to flash them on, but we'll have to make the approach slow. We'll be hanging it all out."

Fetterman said, "Which reaction team are we going to take?"

"Thought that a mix of the best would be ideal. And five of us. One in each ship so that we don't have the same problem that we had this morning." He turned to Lucas. "What's your max load?"

"Vietnamese? Say eight or nine. We're working at night now so that the DA won't affect us."

"DA?"

"Density altitude. How hot and muggy the air is. The hotter it is, the less we can carry. At night, in the cool air, we can carry more. And as we burn off fuel, we can add to the load."

"Okay. Then eight Vietnamese and one American in each load would not be outside the realm of possibility?"

Lucas took a deep breath. He rubbed his face. "I don't know. Nine people. That's an awful big load."

"Can you do it?"

"I suppose."

"Good. That gives us forty-five people."

"How long will you be on the ground?"

"An hour. No more. You can orbit east of the ville. We'll call you when we're ready. The PZ should be secure. We'll have a perimeter set up, and if this works the way it should, they won't have mounted a counterattack by the time you get there."

"Take off time?"

"About an hour. Flight time will be only twenty to twenty-five minutes. We're not going to be able to fly over for a recon. We've got to go straight in and land. Anything else will warn them off."

"Captain," said Fetterman, "that doesn't give us much time to select the reaction team."

"Johnny can get with Bao to select them. You get with Minh. He should be able to give you twenty good men in a couple of minutes. Take them by the ammo bunker and have them draw extra ammo. Each man is going to have to be responsible for his own ammo and equipment. We don't have time to run it any other way.

"As for the aircraft assignments, I'll be in lead and Johnny will be in trail. Sergeant Fetterman will take chock three, Tyme in four, and Smith in two.

"Johnny, I imagine that you'll want Bao in trail with you. Minh should take three. I'm assuming that he'll volunteer."

"Captain," interrupted Bromhead. "You're creating that situation you've tried to avoid. Both of us, and Minh off the camp at one time."

"Special circumstances, Johnny. Besides, with the helicopters, we can get one of us back here in minutes if we have to. And half our team will be in place."

Fetterman said, "Captain, you're really stripping the camp. Minh and Bao too. If something should happen, it's going to be a bad situation."

"I'm aware of that. But this mission is something that can't be put off and the only way that it will work is if we take the top people. Sergeants Bocker and Clarke are capable of handling the defense of the camp. It's a risk that I think we should take.

"We'll use a standard assault on the village, but rather than stopping, we'll sweep on through. Fetterman, your squad will be a point, and we'll be following on the flanks. A triangle-type formation with you at the apex. We don't stop. We don't slow down, but we do take prisoners."

"Captain, weight," said Lucas.

"You'll have burned off an hour's worth of fuel, and I doubt that we'll have all that many prisoners. We can dump the extra ammo in the PZ if we have to."

"Shouldn't Kepler go?" asked Bromhead.

"No. He's been out enough lately, and besides he has work to do here. If we need anything from him, we can call him on the radio."

"He's not going to like being left behind."

"Hell, I don't like going," said one of the pilots. "Let him have my place."

There was a bark of laughter.

Gerber consulted his notes. "Captain Lucas, you'll have to brief your people on any specifics for your end. If you find something that conflicts with the mission, please let me know. If there are no questions?" He waited for a few seconds. "No? Let's go. We'll form up on the choppers in, ah, fifty-nine—no, make it sixty minutes. Each of you will be responsible for the men in your section, both going in and coming out. Make sure they understand that we won't wait for stragglers. We have to stay together and we have to get in and out quickly."

He stopped talking for a moment and then said to Lucas, "If everything goes right tonight, we'll destroy that cadre and you guys can go home in the morning."

"What," said Lucas, "and give up all this?" His wide gesture encompassed the team house and the tent outside it.

"I'm afraid so."

"Well, it's the price paid for success."

There was another burst of laughter.

"If no one has anything else, let's do it."

On the way out of the room Bromhead said, "What happens if we land right on top of the whole company?"

"We're going to have one hell of a fight for a couple of minutes. But we'll be able to get out on the helicopters."

"Unless they get shot down."

"Johnny, you're a real bundle of joy."

CHAPTER 6 _____

Far to the north, both Lucas and Gerber could see a spot of light that looked like a fire burning. Most of the rest of countryside was dark. To the right was one, maybe two lights, and to the left, deep in Cambodia, there seemed to be the glow of a city. But near them, there was nothing except dark gray sky and black ground.

Lucas had entered an orbit as he checked the map. He looked over his shoulder at Gerber and used the intercom to say, "That has to be it. Nothing else around."

"Okay. Let's back off to the east and come in east to west. You can low-level out of there, turn north, and orbit over the river, near the camp. If you don't hear from us, come back in one hour. Land on the north side of the ville, about a klick out. Come in west to east and we'll be ready. If we call, you'll have to come straight in because it will mean that we're getting the shit kicked out of us."

"Do we have suppression going in?"

"Let's not, unless we receive fire. Let's keep them guessing about this."

"Roger that."

Lucas broke out of the orbit and headed east. About twelve klicks from the village, he turned again, trying to spot the fire, but it was now too far away, or hidden among the trees. He stayed at fifteen hundred feet until he saw the fire and then began a gradual descent so that they would arrive at the LZ at little more than two hundred feet. He rolled over to a hundred knots instead of the normal eighty.

There was nothing to see on the ground. It wasn't like flight school in the World where the night was ablaze with a sea of light. Everything from towns and cities to farms and highways. Light everywhere. Light that could be used for navigation, light to tell you where the ground was, and light to reassure you.

Vietnam was different. To show a light at night meant being a target. If the ARVN and VNAF didn't bomb and strafe, then the Americans might. Or the VC would arrive to find out why someone was burning a light. In Vietnam, at night, everyone hated light and tried not to show any—even the Green Berets. They used blackout curtains and light discipline. They said that a match could be seen at two miles if the conditions were right, and Lucas believed it now. The lights in Cambodia had to be twenty or thirty miles away.

And the stars. The numbers and brightness were unbelievable. Instead of the washed-out sky from the World, this one was splattered with thousands of stars. The bright, nearly full moon made it almost possible to read without any other source of light. It was the perfect night for such a mission.

Three klicks out, Lucas said, "We'll be on the ground in less than two minutes. Get ready."

Gerber held up a thumb and peeled off the flight helmet. He buckled on his steel pot, remembering a John Wayne movie where the crusty veteran told the FNG—fucking new guy—that he shouldn't buckle the strap. Shell concussions would pull his head off. But the VC wouldn't be dropping big bombs or large artillery shells, and there was the real possibility that he would lose his helmet when he jumped out of the helicopter.

He locked a magazine in his weapon and injected a round into the chamber. He had his magazines set up with tracers in the first few rounds so that he could see where he was shooting. After that, he hoped to be on the other side of Tuy Dong, and any shooting would be at targets silhouetted against the fires.

The crew chief leaned close to Gerber and yelled, "We're on final."

In turn, Gerber yelled, "Everyone get ready. Lock and load. Remember that we'll have friends out there, so be careful and identify your targets."

Just then, they began the flare. A second later, Gerber saw the landing light stab out momentarily. He felt the skids hit the ground. He jumped out the right side, crouched to one knee, and saw the Vietnamese and Tais follow him.

There was a blast of rotor wash as Lucas pulled pitch and the helicopter vanished in the night. Far to the left, Gerber saw a swarm of green tracers dance into the sky. Gerber couldn't tell if they were close to the flight or not.

Then he was on his feet, jogging toward the village, his rifle aimed at the point of light. The men with him fell into a loose formation behind him. Ten or twelve meters to his right, he could see a second group. They were slightly ahead of him, just as they should be.

A single shot was fired, but he couldn't tell if it was incoming or outgoing. It sounded like an M-1 carbine, but the VC had so many of those that it could have been them as easily as one of the strikers.

To the right was the sudden burst of a machine gun and then two explosions from hand grenades.

Gerber yelled to his men, "Keep moving. Watch your flanks. Watch your flanks."

More firing began, all around him. Some of it was incoming. He could see the green tracers. Shooting from the hip, he tried to put four shots into the muzzle flash of the enemy weapon. He heard a shout but couldn't tell if he had hit the target or merely irritated it.

Gerber was now only twenty or thirty meters from the first hootch. He could see Fetterman and the point enter Tuy Dong, and as they did, they were taken under heavy fire. The one thing that Gerber feared most was happening. The men with Fetterman were diving for the available cover.

Fetterman saw it too and knew what it meant. They would be pinned down and overrun. He turned, saw a VC soldier, and dropped him with a single rifle shot. Then he spun and kicked at one of the Vietnamese, trying to get him moving.

To Minh, shouted, "If they don't move, we leave them. You tell them that."

He kept walking, dodging around the corner of a

hootch. He tossed a grenade behind it and followed it just after it exploded. He was met by a VC guard, bayonet fixed. Fetterman smiled at the man, deflected the blade, and killed him.

In the center of the village, people were screaming. Fetterman ran toward the sound, followed by Minh and two of his Vietnamese sergeants. He pushed past the people there, the civilians forced to stay in the open by the VC. He was acutely aware that he was now silhouetted by the fire and he didn't like the feeling of being naked. He jumped through the door of a hootch and saw a single male with an AK-47. Fetterman grabbed the barrel of the weapon and jerked. The enemy let go. He pulled a knife and leaped for Fetterman's throat, but Fetterman swung the AK one-handed. The blow caught the Viet Cong in the chest, knocking him to the ground. Fetterman stepped close and kicked the man in the chin, snapping his head back. He bent over the VC and realized, by his uniform, that he was one of the cadre. Fetterman tied the unconscious man's hands with a boot lace and threw him over his shoulder.

Outside, there was more shooting. Grenades were popping all over, the majority of them thrown by the VC. Fetterman ran around the hootch and was suddenly masked by darkness. Minh was standing there, firing back into the village, trying to silence a light machine gun. He killed the gunner and wounded the assistant gunner. With that weapon out of operation, Minh turned and ran for the northern edge of Tuy Dong.

Gerber was having good luck keeping his men moving. They were shooting rapidly, but they were trying to choose their targets and were directing most of their fire toward the north.

Behind him, he heard someone scream and turned to see two of the Tais fall. Gerber ran back. One of them was hit in the leg. It didn't look like a serious wound, but it was bleeding freely. Gerber stripped his belt and wrapped it around the leg, pulling it tight. He helped the wounded man to his feet and then waved another of the Tais over to help his friend.

Gerber crouched over the body of the other man. He was obviously dead. The bullet had hit him in the forehead. It was a small, neat hole going in, but a large ragged one coming out. Gerber grabbed the shoulder of the dead man's jungle fatigues, dragging him forward.

The load lightened as someone grabbed the other side, and together they ran through the village.

On the other side of the line, Bromhead was meeting stiff resistance. From the moment they entered the village, they were taken under heavy fire. It became impossible to move, and they were pinned down. To his left he saw that the people there were having the same trouble. He didn't know about Fetterman's group but hoped they, at least, were moving.

Bromhead crawled forward to the edge of a hootch and tried to see where all the shooting was coming from. At the edge of the village near a cluster of trees, he could see a machine gun. Near it were a dozen or more Viet Cong soldiers, all with AK-47s. They were shooting as fast as they could, but all their rounds were going over his head. Bromhead pulled a grenade and tossed it. It fell short by a couple of meters, but the blast surprised the VC. In the lull, Bromhead got to his knees and threw another. It landed in the trees. He threw a third and a fourth. Both fell among the enemy, and suddenly the firing ceased.

"Let's go," he shouted. "Everyone up. Let's go."

He leaped to his feet, ran forward, and collided headlong with an enemy soldier. Both went down. Bromhead was stunned, unable to move. The VC recovered, got to his knees, and used his rifle butt to hit Bromhead. Then he aimed his rifle, but before he pulled the trigger, there was a burst of M-1 carbine fire and Bao was standing over Bromhead, trying to get him on his feet.

"You get up now, Lieutenant Johnny, or we be left."

Shaking his head, Bromhead staggered to his feet, saw that the Tais and Vietnamese were gathered around him.

"Spread out," he yelled. "Move it."

The Tais smiled and began to fan out, but first each one came by to touch Bromhead, as if he was a charm that would guarantee their safety. They might have really believed it.

But there was no time to think about it. Bromhead raced forward, afraid that they would be left by the helicopters. At the edge of the village he turned and saw that all the men who had been on the helicopter with him were gathered near him.

He emptied his magazine into the trees where the machine gun had been hidden. He turned and ran across the swampy ground, looking back to gauge the distance. When he was far enough away, he dropped to the ground, crawled to a large rock, and surveyed the damage.

Tuy Dong was in flames. The thatch of most of the hootches was on fire. He could see a few bodies scattered around, but not many. Tracers were still coming from the village, but the firing was sporadic and undisciplined. Some of the men in the other parties were returning it in a more coordinated fashion.

Bromhead looked at his watch, surprised to find that the hour was nearly up. The choppers would be landing in only a few minutes. He couldn't believe how the time had been compressed by the heat of the battle.

With the extraction from the village finished, he pulled his band closer together and then moved toward the center of the line. He found Fetterman, and they began setting up the perimeter as if they expected a counterattack.

Gerber and his men arrived. "Anyone get a casualty count?"

"Not yet. I think we have everyone."

"Even the dead?"

"Yes sir. We tired to bring them out."

"Good. So did I."

"We got a prisoner," said Fetterman. "I think it's one of the cadre. Found him in a hootch. Should please Kepler no end."

In the distance, Gerber heard the helicopters. "Everyone make a quick check. If we've left anyone, I don't know how we're going to find them."

"I think we've got everyone."

"Get them formed into parties for the choppers. Let's put some rounds into the ville to keep their heads down."

*   *   *

The helicopter extraction was anticlimatic. There was virtually no opposition from the village. The men climbed onto the choppers, which took off in order, having been on the ground for ten seconds or less. Once airborne, Gerber counted and found that everyone he had brought out in his aircraft was in it again. Two of them were dead, and one wounded. He asked Lucas to poll the rest of the flight. There were an additional five dead and seven wounded, but everyone was there.

With that information, Gerber took off the helmet and set it on the floor near his feet. He leaned against the soundproofing and closed his eyes, relaxing for the first time since Kepler had told him that the VC propaganda cadre would be in Tuy Dong. They hadn't destroyed the cadre but they had put a dent in its operation. Then he realized that the information supplied by the young prisoner had been right on the mark.

In camp, McMillan waited at the north end of the runway with a platoon of strikers who held stretchers. As the flight landed, the stretcher bearers advanced and picked up the wounded and the dead. McMillan hustled them all to the dispensary for immediate treatment. He didn't wait for Gerber or Bromhead to tell him what to do.

As soon as he had gotten a look at the wounds and treated those who needed immediate attention, he got on the field phone and told Bocker that he wanted an medical evacuation as soon as possible for the more seriously wounded. None was in danger, but they all needed treatment and a couple needed to have bullets removed.

That done, and with no one in immediate danger of dying, McMillan, and Thomas Jefferson Washington, the other Green Beret medical specialist, held a sick call for those with minor injuries. Bromhead was one of the first, complaining of a headache and double vision.

McMillan gave him some aspirin and told him to get some rest, but if he still had double vision in the morning to come back.

From there they treated a variety of burns, cuts, and bruises. After two hours, they had finished and were cleaning up.

Gerber swung by to see how the injured were. The evac helicopters had come and gone. When he saw that things had slowed, he said, "I think we should go out to Tuy Dong tomorrow and see if we can render any aid. That is, once we fly a recon to make sure that the VC have left."

McMillan, feeling the strain of being awake most of the night and then having to treat the wounded, slumped onto a stool near one of the medical cabinets. He leaned on it. "If what we had here is a sample of what we'd see, I think we'll need to get a full medical team. A doctor and nurses."

"You can't handle it?"

"I didn't say that. But I'm assuming that you'll want the best treatment for those people and I'm not a doctor. Besides, I don't have enough medicine for that."

"So we'll call for a medical team."

"Now?" asked McMillan.

"Now. Somebody will be awake at Nha Trang. If

they put them on a Caribou, they could be here in plenty of time. We could run the recon while they're en route."

"Okay, Captain, I'll call Nha Trang, but they're not going to like it."

"They never do, and they don't have to. Let me know what you find out."

Kepler had the captured VC cadre man sitting with him in the team house. Two of the Tais stood close by, guarding him. Kepler knew that he would get nothing out of the man. He wasn't a youngster like the one who had talked the day before. He was a trained agent who was aware of all the tricks that could be played, all the tortures that could be used, and who understood the value of the slightest piece of information. He wouldn't be fooled by kindness.

They sat opposite one another. Finally, to break the ice, Kepler said, "What's your name?"

The man continued his hostile stare.

"I suppose it will do no good to tell you that telling me your name will hurt no one."

At that moment, Gerber entered and glanced at Kepler, who shrugged. "I suggest we put this guy on a plane to Saigon as soon as we can. We'll get nothing out of him."

"I'll have Bocker make the request in a few minutes. If you've got some time, I need to talk to you."

Outside, away from the team house, they stopped. Gerber put one foot up on a sandbag and stared into the east where it was just beginning to turn light. "We hurt that propaganda team last night, but we didn't destroy it. Your friend in there may, or may not, be a part of it. At the very least, he was a high-ranking member of the escort."

"Why do you say that?"

"We got him in the ville, not in the boonies with the guards. You can't get anything out of him?"

"Oh, I suppose, after three, four days, if we used sleep deprivation, refused to feed him, we might. But he strikes me as a real fanatic. Some of those people will sit there and watch you cut off fingers or hands, and smile. They will die happily, knowing that they have defeated you."

"I thought anyone could be made to talk," said Gerber.

"About ninety-nine percent can, but once in a while, you get a fanatic. There's not much you can do, except not waste your time. We've got a valuable intelligence asset in that young boy, though."

"I think you're right about one thing," said Gerber. "We should keep the kid around for a couple of days at least. That other guy. Let's get him out of here before he causes us trouble."

"Have we given up on capturing that propaganda cadre, Captain?"

"No. Why do you ask?"

"We had a chance tonight and didn't take it."

"No, Derek, we didn't. There wasn't the time to put a force in the field that would have allowed us to do that. We had time to disrupt the meeting, but we couldn't capture them. Their guard force was too strong."

"They'll strengthen it now if they continue to use it."

"Of course they will, and that will make our victory that much more impressive. But we have to know where they'll be well in advance so that we can get enough people into the field to meet them."

"That means I'll have to use the chief's daughter. Even if the prisoner knew what the schedule was, I'm sure they'll change it."

"I suppose you're right. You'll have to begin the process of getting her used to you. Work with her so that she's not afraid. I can't see anything else to do."

"First thing in the morning."

"This is first thing in the morning," said Gerber, checking his watch and smiling.

Feeling that his work was never done, Gerber walked across the airfield looking for Captain Lucas. He found him standing on the ground in front of a helicopter, looking up at the rotor blade. The crew chief was on top of the aircraft, closely inspecting a bullet hole.

"It's just a hole. Didn't hit the spar?"

"No sir. Looks like it went through clean. I don't think it weakened the blade at all."

"Okay. Climb down. We'll have maintenance look at it when we get the chance. The replacement ships arrive?"

"First thing tomorrow. They're bringing out two. They'll fly the others back."

"Speaking of first thing in the morning," said Gerber, "We need a recon flight over Tuy Dong. First to check damage and second to see if the enemy is still there."

"Single ship?"

"Unless you think more are necessary. We want to put some medical people into the ville to help the populace there. We'll want a reaction team close, maybe two lifts so that we'll have plenty of people around in case the medical team needs help.''

''What time?''

''Recon would be nice as soon as it's light enough to see. The medical team won't be here for several hours. We could have the reaction force in place, by, say, ten. Any problems?''

''No. We've got a couple of replacement ships coming in, but they should be here before eight. We'll need to refuel and rearm before we start any serious missions.''

''You know what you need,'' said Gerber. ''Figure on one recon flight, two full lifts, and then a partial with the medical folks.''

''You want to go on the recon flight?''

''No. Take Sergeant Fetterman. He'll know what to look for.''

''We'll let you know before we go.''

CHAPTER 7_____

The luck of the draw was not with Ramsey or Chrisman. They got the rare and distinct privilege of flying Sergeant Fetterman on the recon mission. Ramsay accepted the news with his normal aplomb. He threw his chicken plate to the floor and would have kicked it, but the last time he did that, he nearly broke his toe.

"Must be that Lucas hates us. Either him or God. Otherwise they would send someone else."

"No big thing," said Chrisman, picking up his pistol and helmet.

"It is when you've gotten as much flight time in the last few days as we have. Did you know there was an army regulation that limited you to eight hours in one day and no more than ninety in a thirty-day period?"

"So what?"

"So we've already busted those. And we're going to get more."

Chrisman burst into laughter. "You about through?"

"Yeah," said Ramsey, laughing. "I'm all through."

"Then we'd better get out to the aircraft and preflight. Besides, the recon shouldn't take that long."

"You know, Fred, sometimes your optimism is sickening."

"Yes, but if it wasn't for that, you'd probably poison the thinking of the whole company. I'm a good balance for you."

"Okay, balance, why don't you balance your butt out to the flight line while I get a cup of coffee."

Fetterman was cleaning his weapon when Tyme arrived. He said, "I understand you're going on the recon."

"True."

"Want some help?"

"What's wrong, Boom-Boom? You lonesome or something?"

"No, not really. I just wanted to see how badly we shot up that ville last night."

"Then grab your gear and let's go. I'll have this back together in a minute."

When they arrived at the helicopter, the rotor blades were already turning. Both Fetterman and Tyme ran across the open area and leaped into the back. Fetterman took off his steel pot and replaced it with the helmet hooked into the intercom. Over that he said, "We're set."

They picked up to a hover, moved forward out of the revetment, and turned to the south, taking off into the light breeze there. Immediately they climbed to fifteen hundred feet.

"Only a few minutes," said Ramsey. "We'll fly over once at altitude and let you guys scope out the situation. Then I'll come around and pass over at low altitude. Finally, as a test, we'll orbit a couple of times in a slight climb. If there are any VC there, they should fire at us. The first round we take, I break down and away and we come back here."

Before they got close, they spotted the village. It was easy because of the pillar of dark smoke. It was about the only thing in the area that could burn since most of it was surrounded by swamp.

They approached rapidly. Just as Ramsey had said, they flew over at fifteen hundred feet. Fetterman could see the remains of ten or twelve hootches, but the smoke was pouring out of one near the center as if someone had set a half-dozen old tires on fire.

There appeared to be a couple of bodies lying among the hootches and another at the edge of the village. Two were dressed in black pajamas while the third wore only black shorts.

There was no sign of movement below them, other than one water buffalo that was running loose among the hootches.

When they were a klick south, Ramsay made a rapid descent, turned, and came back. He circled to the west and made his pass to the east. It was just like he said it would be. Low and fast.

Again, there was nothing moving in the village. A couple of small fires were burning on the edge of the trees. Fetterman thought he saw movement there but couldn't tell whether it was the smoke, or human.

Now they popped up to a thousand feet and turned to the left to begin the orbit. Fetterman slid across the troop seat so he could see out the door. Below him the village was apparently deserted. It was going to make it hard for them to render aid if they couldn't find the villagers. Thinking about it, he realized that the VC could recover some of their lost ground by evacuating the villagers, telling them that they weren't safe. After all, it had been the American and South Vietnamese attackers who had started the firefight.

They orbited four times, long enough for any VC to open fire. But no one shot at them. Smoke drifted over the village, and a lone water buffalo, frightened by the helicopter, crashed off into the swamp.

Ramsey came over the intercom and said, "You seen enough?"

"Yes, plenty."

Back at the camp, Gerber listened to Fetterman's report and shook his head. "That was about the last thing I expected."

"Well, Captain, there are a couple of possibilities. One is, as I said, the VC took them into Cambodia. Can't really believe that, because the VC wouldn't want to be encumbered with a bunch of villagers.

"Two is that the people heard the helicopter and ran to hide. We saw the one large fire, but most of everything else had burned out. The small fires could have been for cooking."

"Kind of shoots my plan all to hell. I had wanted to send in the medical team with very little support, keeping our troops at a distance. Now I suppose we ought to sweep through. Keep the medical people at the rear of the formation."

Fetterman set his steel pot on a table. "I think those people are out there."

"Get Minh's reaction team, no make it Bao's. We'll put them down a klick or so from the ville. Have Minh's get ready to sweep and to provide security."

"Yes sir."

The plane carrying the medical personnel landed, taxied, and stopped. The door opened and ten men and women wearing clean and pressed jungle fatigues emerged. Gerber had expected white coats for no good reason. He could tell that some of them were medical people, though, because they carried scissors stuck through the pocket flap of their shirts.

There was a tall, thin major with short dark, slicked-down hair in the lead and he was carrying a olive-drab rucksack with a red cross on it. He walked to Gerber and said, "We're here."

Gerber said, "Let's go to the team house for some coffee. I want to put some troops in near the ville before we go in. I don't like the way this is shaping up. You might want to have a couple of your people go over to the dispensary." He gestured to McMillan. "Doc, you want to show them where to go."

He turned back to the major. "This is Sergeant McMillan, our senior medical specialist."

The major stuck out his hand. "I'm Dr. Acalotta. I think that Lieutenant Denton and Lieutenant Hodges would be happy to go to the dispensary, Sergeant."

McMillan moved to the right and said, "Follow me." Two of the nurses dropped out of the group. Both carried scissors and small rucksacks with red crosses. Over his shoulder he said to them, "Any help you can provide will be greatly appreciated. It isn't often that we get professional medical assistance here."

In the dispensary, McMillan said, "My name's Ian. Any questions, please ask. Any suggestions, please make them."

They checked the dressings on the wounded, took blood pressure, and listened to hearts. They stared into Bromhead's eyes to make sure the pupils were the same size since he had received a head injury. That done, they complimented McMillan on his operation, saying it was the best they had seen in the field. They didn't tell him it was the only one they had seen in the field.

He motioned them to sit down and then said, "Can I ask a favor? I have one more patient, but I'm not sure what to do with her."

The taller nurse, the one with the red hair who said her name was Louise Denton, said, "We're here to help."

McMillan told them the whole story then, watching them carefully. Both reacted with horror when they heard what had been done to the chief's daughter. Both wanted to help.

"So far," said McMillan, "I'm the only one who has been able to get close to her. She retreats from everyone else, but I haven't had female assistance until now. How should we handle it?"

Denton said, "I suppose that we could just walk in. You might want to stay in the background while we make an examination. If she reacts violently, you might be able to calm her."

They opened the door and entered. The young Vietnamese girl didn't look at them. She continued staring at the ceiling. McMillan said quietly, "I've brought some nurses to help you."

Denton moved close to the bed and took the girl's hand. She looked at Denton and her eyes widened briefly. Then she sobbed once and buried her face on Denton's shoulder. She began to cry uncontrollably.

Hodges touched McMillan. "Let's leave. Your patient seems to be responding to Louise."

"I'll say."

In the team house, Major Acalotto and Gerber discussed the mission. Gerber unfolded a map and showed it to Acalotto. "We'll be going in here. We had a firefight with the VC last night, and from our recon this morning, the enemy seems to have left. The villagers seem to be gone too, although we did see some signs of life. All we really want is for someone to treat any injuries of the people. If someone is hurt badly, we can bring them back here or have them evacked to Saigon."

"You want my nurses to go into the field?"

"Well, you have two in the dispensary. We'll have nearly a hundred troops in the field. Forty with you and another forty on standby just outside the ville. And everyone here. You should be safe enough."

"When do we go?"

"Just as soon as I can get the first lift in."

While everyone was busy setting up the mission into the village, Kepler visited Thanh in the locked storage room. He took him some breakfast and a cup of water.

"I've done what you asked," said Kepler. "You'll

remain here for a while. But you've got to help me. I do you a favor and now you owe me one."

Thanh had been eating almost as fast as he could stuff the food into his mouth. He stopped now and asked, "What can I do for you?"

Kepler had reached the critical stage. A wrong move could blow it and undermine Thanh's usefulness. He didn't want to treat Thanh as an idiot, but he was young and immature. Kepler was walking a thin line. He had to be careful.

"All we need to do is talk a little bit. You don't have to discuss military information. I mean, yesterday you told me about the cadre living on your base, and I told you about some of the problems we face. No one was hurt, but my captain was impressed with that. That's why he said you could stay here. But I have to report that we are continuing our discussions."

"I still don't know what I can do." Thanh had begun eating again.

"Well, take that cadre, for example. Do they have a regular schedule, or is it hit and miss."

"They didn't come in until about three weeks ago. They only said that we should stay out of their way and that they would be talking to villagers."

"Where were they going after Tuy Dong?"

"Ap Tan." Thanh's hand froze halfway to his mouth. He realized that he had been tricked.

Kepler laughed. "Hey, don't worry about. I have something to tell the captain. He'll be happy, and you can stay. If you need anything, let me know."

Kepler found Gerber just as he was going to get on a helicopter with the medical team. He said, "Before you take off, Captain, can I talk to you?"

"What about?"

"I think I know where that cadre is going to be next."

"How?"

"Thanh told me. Apparently the cadre has some kind of route and their next target is Ap Tan."

"You really think they'll go there after last night?"

Behind them, the flight cranked, filling the air with the whine of the turbines and the smell of JP-4.

Over the noise, Kepler said, "They just might. Maybe they figure that we were drawn by the bonfire. Maybe we can get in there without them knowing it."

Gerber glanced at the helicopters. "I've got to go."

"Yes sir. What about the propaganda cadre?"

"I don't know. I just don't think we can expect them to stick to their schedule now."

"But if they did, we'd look pretty stupid. I mean, we know where they said they would be. Why not put someone into the field to spy on them. If we can get into place first, we'll have a real shot at taking them out."

"Why don't you get with Fetterman and see what the two of you can come up with. We'll be back in a couple of hours. Have something ready for me then."

The flight landed near Tuy Dong without incident. Minh and his reaction team secured the area and began the sweep toward the village. Gerber and the medical team, which included Sergeant Washington, were near the center of the formation.

As they approached, they couldn't see any movement in the village. The big fire had gone out, but there was still smoke.

A few of Minh's men ran forward to a couple of the hootches and then entered them. They were inside for two or three minutes searching for hidden bunkers and tunnels, but they found nothing. The hootches were empty, and that in itself was strange. There should have been, at the very least, a straw sleeping mat and a black pot.

The sweep continued, with the Vietnamese searching each of the hootches. Toward the center of the village they found evidence of the assault. Bullet holes in the mud walls and some blood patches on the ground. In one, there was a broken stock from an AK-47. In another was a bloody black pajama bottom. Scattered around were the empty shell casings from the M-14s, AK-47s, M-1s, and the machine guns. A couple of unexploded Chinese grenades were found inside one hootch.

But the people were all gone. So were the animals. There was no sign of life, and if it hadn't been for the fires and the shell casings, Gerber would have been convinced that they were in the wrong place. Even the bodies seen by Fetterman were missing.

"I thought you said there were injured people here," said Acalotto.

"I thought there would be."

"Didn't you fly a recon?"

"Of course. I told you that. But it was looking for signs of enemy, not for the villagers. Sergeant Fetterman said that he hadn't seen anyone, but the assumption was that they were hiding because of last night."

At the far end of Tuy Dong, one of the Vietnamese found a small boy hiding under a bush. The man tried to coax the kid out, and when that failed, he kicked at him. The boy only crawled out of range, whimpering.

Minh called, "Over here, old boy."

Gerber and Acalotto ran over. Gerber pushed the Vietnamese trooper out of the way. He got down on his hands and knees and tried to talk to the boy. But the boy just hid his eyes and pretended that he was alone.

Gerber then crawled under the bush, and the boy retreated, into the waiting arms of Minh, who said, in Vietnamese, "It's all right now. You're safe."

The boy was badly burned on his legs and one arm. He had several superficial cuts on his face and neck. One of the nurses took the boy and set him on the ground. She opened her rucksack and started spreading salve on his burns.

"A couple of second-degree," she said, "but most of them are minor."

Minh moved close to Gerber and whispered to him. "We've found some fresh-turned earth over there. I think we may have found the villagers."

"Oh, Christ. You don't think they . . ."

"I've told a couple of my chaps to take a look. We'll know then."

Gerber smiled at the Vietnamese officer, thinking that it was strange to hear him speak with such a clipped British accent. But the British education and military training were a real asset. Most South Vietnamese officers with professional training had been educated in France. "Let's go take a look."

Three of the soldiers were digging with entrenching tools, throwing the dirt into the trees. One of them exposed a hand and another found a foot.

To himself Gerber said, "Well, we've found the people."

A moment later, they had two bodies, a young woman and an old man. Each had been shot several times in the head and chest.

Acalotto, coming up from behind, misinterpreted what he saw. "What in the hell are you people doing? Leave those people alone."

"We found the villagers. The VC murdered them."

"Oh sure," said Acalotto. "The VC did it."

Gerber spun, the anger rising in him. What he was seeing was making him sick, and now to be accused, by a deskbound, rear-echelon doctor was too much.

"You think I would do this? You think I would kill all these people? Why? And why would I bring you and your people here as witnesses? Don't you even begin to think that I would do this."

"Sorry Captain."

"Captain Gerber," said Lieutenant Minh, "one of my men has said that the boy told him a few of the people escaped into the swamp last night. After we swept through, the VC rounded them all up and shot them. Buried them quickly and ran away."

"Let's get some security set."

"Should we look for the villagers?"

"No. It will be useless. They'll stay out there until we leave. They're going to be afraid of everyone," said Gerber.

"What about us?" asked Acalotto.

"Hang loose." Gerber turned to the RTO—the radio telephone operator. He took the mike and called Tyme, who was with Bao to the south. "Sweep through on line and pick up anyone you see. Be careful. We've seen no sign of the enemy, but that doesn't mean they aren't there."

An hour later, Tyme, Bao, and the reaction force entered the village. They had found two old men and one old woman. They were all frightened, but not so frightened that they couldn't repeat what they had seen. They said that the attack the previous night angered the Viet Cong. The VC lost twenty or more killed and a like number wounded. Only a few of the villagers were hurt since most of them had hidden as soon as the shooting started. When the attack was over, the VC rounded up everyone, forced them into the center of the village, and began shooting them. A lot of them tried to run, and some of them made it. Just after dawn, the VC burned the hootches and left.

By this time, Minh's men had uncovered forty-two bodies, most of them women and children. Gerber told them to stop searching. They knew all they had to.

"Cover and bodies," he said. "It's all we can do for them." He then got on the radio and ordered in the helicopters. To Minh he said, "Normally, I would take one of the groups back on a patrol to see if we can find anyone else, but there is something else building that we might have to act on tonight. Let's just get out of here."

Walking back to the center of the village, Gerber saw one of the nurses standing by a hootch, holding the bloody pajama bottoms and crying. He put a hand on her shoulder.

"How could they do something like that? Why?"

"I guess they didn't want the people to know that they had failed to such an extent," said Gerber.

"You mean the VC killed everyone because they might look bad?"

"I'm afraid so."

She stared at Gerber. "Then you're partly responsible. If you hadn't come last night, these people would be alive."

"I'm afraid so," he repeated.

"How can you live with that?"

Gerber moved his hand away. "I don't have to. What I did was right. I had no way of knowing that the VC would react that way. I didn't . . ."

She was crying harder. "Just get away from me."

Gerber started away and then looked back. He saw that she was leaning against the mud wall, one hand over her eyes as her shoulders shook. She was wrong, thought Gerber. It was the VC who had committed the atrocity, not Gerber, or the Special Forces, or the men working with them. It was a VC terror tactic. In fact, they would probably use this as an example of the power of the VC in the south. The Americans had been unable to protect Tuy Dong. And the fact that the Americans had not been trying to protect the village would be lost in the telling of the tale.

No, Gerber had not been wrong. He knew that. But there was no way that he would be able to convince the nurse. She just couldn't see war for what it was. She was too isolated from the realities of the situation. She thought war was two armies in brightly colored uniforms fighting each other on a field of honor. She didn't know that this war was fought without front lines, with everyone, no matter how old, no matter what sex, as a participant. Maybe some didn't want to be involved, but until one side or the other quit, the people would be caught in the middle.

Gerber shook his head and walked back to where Bao and Tyme were discussing where to place the last of the security force. He said to them, "I've called for the helicopters."

CHAPTER 8

The meeting in the team house was only for Gerber, Fetterman, Tyme, Kepler, and Minh. Everyone else was going about his duties, with the exception of the medical people. They all had gone over to the dispensary to offer what help they could. There were only a couple of sick and wounded there, and that included the few people they brought out of the village. Louise Denton was still with the chief's daughter, but had gotten her to talk and to agree to meet with Kepler.

Fetterman had a giant chart spread out on a table. One corner was held down by a can of C-rations, one corner by a Randall combat knife, and one with a pistol. The last one curled up now and then, but Fetterman tried to lean on it to keep it straight.

"As you can see, Ap Tan isn't more than twenty, twenty-five klicks from here. And according to the map, it's a fairly big village, maybe two, three hundred people."

131

"What do you want to do?"

Now Kepler took over. "We do know that Thanh's information last night was good. He told us that the VC propaganda cadre would be moving into Ap Tan for another meeting.

"There are two schools of thought on this. One is that the VC will change their plans, afraid that they have been compromised, which they have. Or they can assume that our arrival was a fluke and everything will stay on schedule.

"Looking over the chart and by getting some more information from Thanh, we know that the cadre likes to get into the village during the day, spend that talking to the people, and then hold a meeting at night. They have varied this, spending as many as three days in one place."

Kepler took a pencil from his pocket. He pointed to Ap Tan. "By studying the map, we can see that it will take them two days at a minimum to get to Ap Tan. If they return to their base camp, it could be four or five."

"So we have some time?"

"Just wait, Captain," said Fetterman.

"What we would like to do," said Kepler, "is put a small team into the field tonight. They could move toward the ville, find a good place to wait, and observe. When the cadre arrives, the team'll be able to direct the helicopters in to the most advantageous zone."

Fetterman took over. "We could put a large patrol into the field too, with the ultimate destination of Ap Tan. A little coordination will put everyone together at the ville at the same time."

"And do what?"

"Crush the VC company guarding the cadre and capture them."

Gerber moved around so that he could study the map. Unlike Tuy Dong, which had been situated on dry ground in the middle of a swampy area, Ap Tan was to the north. The map indicated high grass and trees bordering on the beginnings of jungle. Plenty of concealment.

"We could send a helicopter over to see what is there."

"I thought of that," said Fetterman, "and decided against it. First, we'll have the time to do that on the ground, and once we get in there, it might be nice to have an overflight once or twice. Too many flights and we could scare the cadre off. It seemed unnecessary at this point."

"Who's on the first team in?"

"I thought I would go in with Lieutenant Minh," said Kepler. "We'd take four others from one of the strike companies."

"Then who will interrogate your prisoner or work with the chief's daughter."

"Well, if we can convince Major Acalotto, I think he ought to leave Lieutenant Denton here for a few days. She's developed quite a relationship with the girl."

"It's only been six hours."

"But the girl seems to have attached herself to Denton. I don't claim to understand it and neither does the doc. He said it might be because Denton was the first woman she saw, after, well, you know . . ."

"She's not going to make much of an agent."

"If she continues to snap out of this the way she

has been, doc said she could go home in two, three days. All I ever wanted was to have her home, watching for signs of the cadre.''

"I think it would be better for Fetterman to go out with the first group," said Gerber. "You have to much to do here, Derek."

"All right, sir. Then Sergeant Fetterman and Minh and those guys would patrol in and set up. I could lead the other team, leaving in two days, if the indications are we have that kind of time."

"How big a force?"

"Forty or fifty. Large enough so that when we hit the VC, we'll be on about an even foot. We'll have surprise, and people in place. Plus the forty coming in by air."

"Okay, let's do it. Tony, you check with me before you take off. I'll tell Lucas that we need one final lift today."

When the meeting ended, Kepler strolled over to the dispensary to check on the chief's daughter. He was surprised to see her sitting in a chair in the outer room of the dispensary. The change was startling.

McMillan stood up and said, "Come on in and meet Anh Co Duan."

Kepler nodded and bowed slightly. "Pleased to meet you," he said in Vietnamese.

She inclined her head and said, in English, "The pleasure is mine."

Kepler raised an eyebrow and McMillan explained. "She has been to school in Saigon. Learned English there."

Pulling a chair to him, Kepler sat down. Duan was wearing a white hospital gown. The high neck covered her chest, but the opening down the back showed some of the cuts when she turned to talk to the others. Her long and graceful legs were bare. Bruises around her knees showed where the ropes had been drawn taut.

"How are you feeling?" asked Kepler.

"Fine. A little sore and my back is itching, but your doctor said it was because it was healing."

Kepler looked at McMillan, who shrugged. "She and Lieutenant Denton had a long talk earlier."

Now Kepler stood and moved to the door. He motioned McMillan to follow. "If you'll excuse us?"

"Certainly."

Outside, Kepler said, "How is she? Really?"

"It's one of the most amazing things I've ever seen. One minute she was practically catatonic, and the next she has opened up completely."

"When can I talk to her about going home and watching for the VC for us?"

"I would prefer that you didn't, but if she hasn't shown any signs of regressing by tomorrow, I suppose then. In fact, though I hate to admit it, it might be a good thing for her. Make her think that she is doing something to avenge the deaths of her family."

They were interrupted by Major Acalotto. He said, "Is Lieutenant Denton in there?"

"Yes sir."

"Thanks." Acalotto opened the door and stepped in. He said, "Louise, you have any objection to staying here tonight?"

Duan jumped in. "Oh, please. We could have such a nice talk."

"No sir. Sure don't," said the nurse.

"All right then. We'll be taking off in about an

hour. See you at the airstrip before we go. Captain Gerber has assured me that you'll be safe here and that he can get you back to our, uh, base tomorrow." He had almost said Nha Trang, but caught himself. He couldn't see any point in telling any of the Vietnamese patients where they were stationed.

At sixteen hundred, Fetterman, Minh, Sergeant Krung, who had been borrowed from Bao, and three strikers were standing at the north end of the airstrip, waiting for their flight.

Gerber came up as the helicopter was cranking. "You ready?"

"Of course."

Gerber looked at the pile of equipment and supplies. "Isn't that an awful lot?"

"We'll be out three days and maybe four. Want to have enough. Besides, the C-rations don't add that much weight, especially when you throw out all the bullshit the army packs into them. We're only taking the good stuff. No ham and lima beans for Mrs. Fetterman's favorite sergeant."

"We'll listen for you to break squelch every night at eighteen hundred and midnight. If you get into trouble, you call. Someone will be monitoring at all times."

"Got it," said Fetterman.

"Kepler and Tyme will be coming out in two days, unless you alert us to send them earlier." Gerber held out his hand. "Good luck and good hunting."

Fetterman shook the hand. "Thanks, Captain. See you in a couple of days."

*   *   *

It seemed like it was only minutes later when the helicopter landed in a rice paddy that was nearly surrounded by trees. Fetterman and Minh jumped out into water that was nearly knee deep. As the helicopter lifted, they were splashing their way up to the trees. Fetterman dropped to the ground near a bush while the others moved into the treeline. He covered them as they set up security, and checked for signs of the enemy. That finished, Fetterman moved into the trees with them.

"I suggest that we move out of here as quickly as possible," said Fetterman.

"I agree, old boy," said Minh.

Sergeant Krung took the point, followed by two of the strikers, Minh, the other striker, and then Fetterman. Normally he would have been in the lead with Krung, but Fetterman knew these people well and trusted them as much as he trusted anyone who wasn't an American.

Krung, on orders, stuck to rice paddy dikes and paths. They weren't worried about boobytraps in this area. Charlie wouldn't have scattered them yet because, for a long time, this territory had been almost exclusively VC. That had changed with the insertion of Camp A-555, but the enemy still roamed with relative impunity. And by staying to the paths and dikes, they wouldn't be leaving obvious traces. The VC might not learn they were in the area.

As the sun set, they stopped for a rest and something to eat. Krung and the Vietnamese ate cold rice "sweetened" with fish heads. Minh, having gotten used to Western food while studying in England, had opted for boned chicken from a C-ration meal. He salted it liberally to improve the taste.

Fetterman had a can of beans and franks. They couldn't risk a fire, so he had to eat them cold, but they were a lot better than ham and lima beans. Fetterman always traded those to the Vietnamese, who had a perverse liking for them. He couldn't understand it, but he made use of it.

After the meal, with the sun gone and the ground dark, they moved out. In the distance, they could see a single light, from a lantern, indicating they were near a farmer's hootch. They steered well clear of it. Later, they heard some talking, but Minh said it was only a farmer and his son talking about planting rice sometime in the near future.

At midnight they halted for a rest. Fetterman turned on his radio, clicked the mike switch twice, telling Gerber that they were all right, and then switched off. After a short rest, they started forward again. Now Fetterman was on the point, using his compass to direct the line of march. He hoped to be close to Ap Tan by morning. Then they would scout the immediate area, find a good spot to hide, and lie low.

After dinner, McMillan took Louise Denton back to the dispensary. They spent·an hour talking to Anh Co Duan. Just before she went to bed, they examined her back and chest, checking for infection and healing. Some of the cuts were now just lines on her skin. The scabs on others were beginning to peel. She laughed at their concern, telling them that she was fine now.

Alone in the outer room of the dispensary, McMillan said, "I can't tell you enough how much I appreciate your help, Lieutenant. You've worked a miracle with Anh Co."

"It was nothing. I think if June had gone in first, Anh Co would have reacted to her. And you can call me Louise now that we're alone."

"Thank you, Louise. And I think you're wrong. You showed a real empathy for Anh Co. It's not something that all the people around here have. I know a lot of folks who can't stomach working with the Vietnamese."

"I know what you mean, and after today, I can understand it."

"But I'm not talking about the VC. I'm talking about the people," said McMillan.

"I didn't say that I condoned it. I said I understood it. I mean, think about it. First of all, you never know who your enemy is. Then you see some of the things they do to each other, like wipe out a village because leaving them alive might spread the report of your failure."

"We're talking about people. I think a lot of it is racial prejudice, but since we're involved in a war, it can be disguised as a hatred of the enemy."

Denton smiled at McMillan. "I don't want to have to sit here and defend a point of view that I don't hold."

"All right, then we'll drop it. Would you care for something to drink?"

"What do you have?"

McMillan opened a cabinet with a key. "I have a fifth of medicinal Beam's. Do you need ice?"

"What, and let it melt in there diluting all that good medicine? Are you crazy?"

"You know what you're doing," said McMillan, pouring a stiff shot into a clean glass.

Denton took it and gulped half of it down. She breathed out through her mouth and said, "That's smooth. We don't get anything like this at Nha Trang."

"That's probably because you always hang out with those stuffy doctor types who think they're being clever by drinking rubbing alcohol."

"Ian, can I ask you a personal question?"

"I suppose, if I can retain my right not to answer."

"What are you doing here?"

"You know that. I'm part of a—"

"No, I mean, why are you in the army? I've watched you work in here and you're as good as any doctor I've seen. It's a real waste of your talent."

McMillan poured himself another drink and set the bottle on the rough wooden table near him. He took one swallow and then said, "I don't see it as a waste of talent. I'm practicing medicine, treating people who really need my help. I like to think that having me here has saved some lives. Sure, I've overstepped my training by performing operations like removing bullets, but if I hadn't, some of those people would have died."

He took a final drink. "No, I don't see it as a waste. In the World, I wouldn't be allowed to do any of the things I'm doing here. I would be stuck driving an ambulance or being some kind of technician."

He smiled to himself. "Did you see how the captain treated me? Asked my opinion. Same with Kepler. They respect my talent. They respect my ability. I'm not some second-rate medic to them. I'm their doctor.

"But it's more than that too. Because we're all professional soldiers here. We're doing a necessary job and we're doing it the right way. We have to fight for every scrap of assistance because the jerks in Saigon don't realize what's happening here. They haven't grasped the finer points of the war. They think in terms of World War II, where you fought the enemy, beat him, and pushed him back. They don't realize that here we need the support of the people to win, and that's what we're doing here. We're showing the people that someone cares about them."

"Wow," said Denton.

"Sorry, I didn't mean to get on my soapbox. But I wanted you to understand that I don't see me as wasting my life here."

"It's been a long day," she said.

McMillan, misunderstanding her, said, "Oh, I'm sorry. You shouldn't let me go on like that."

She put her glass down. "Do you find me unattractive?"

"Of course not." McMillan suddenly understood. He got to his feet and leaned over her. He kissed her once, on the forehead and then his lips found hers.

She put her hand up, on his neck, as if she was holding his head in place. Then she broke the kiss and said, "This is so public."

Together they moved to another room, at the back of the dispensary. Inside, McMillan had to set up a cot. That finished, he sat down and said, "I'm sorry about how this is going."

Denton, who had unbuttoned the top of her jungle fatigues, looked slightly hurt. "What does that mean?"

"It means"—McMillan took her hand—"that I would like to have a beautiful room, filled with wine and food for you. That I find you to be a beautiful, intelligent woman who deserves something more than an army cot and a waterglass of Beam's Choice. I mean, that I find you to be a special person, and I don't want to offend you.''

She stepped close to him and took his head in both her hands so that he could kiss her bare stomach. ''That's a beautiful thought,'' she said.

Finally she moved away from him, took off her jacket, and began unbuttoning her pants. She slipped them over her hips and then sat down to take them off. She stood again, moving toward the door as if she wanted to make sure that it was closed, but what she was doing was showing off. She wanted McMillan to inspect her. To look at her.

McMillan sat on the cot and looked. He watched her do something with her hair, piled on her head as regulations demanded, so that it hung down to her shoulders. He looked at her long, thin legs that were lightly tanned, thanks to free time on the beaches of Nha Trang. The wisp of cloth around her hips that masqueraded as panties did little to hide her. They made her look just that much more desirable.

She moved back and let him feel her again. She pressed her stomach close to his face, and when she felt his hand on her inner thigh, she trembled and spread her legs for him.

''I want to make love to you,'' she said. ''I need to make love.''

An hour before dawn, Fetterman found himself on a slight rise looking down on the village of Ap Tan. It would be the perfect place for observing the settlement, and that was the trouble with it. The VC would be inclined to put people on the hill once they arrived, and there wasn't enough cover to hide from them. Fetterman would have to find somewhere else.

Below them, people were already awake and moving. Cooking fires were burning brightly. Everything looked so peaceful and normal that Fetterman was instantly suspicious. Then he decided that he was being paranoid. If the VC were there, they were being very careful. And if they were there, they also didn't know that Fetterman and his group had arrived. If they had known, Fetterman would have seen some sign of it. He saw none.

CHAPTER 9

SPECIAL FORCES CAMP A-555

The five helicopters, their rotors spinning, sat on the north end of the earth runway, churning up great clouds of red dust. Standing twenty meters to the left were five groups of ten men. Tyme was with the first of these and Smith with the last.

The helicopters had already flown a number of missions that day so that the fuel load was substantially reduced. Lucas had said if the weather cooperated and they had a smaller fuel load, then carrying nine or ten of the Vietnamese might be possible. Gerber had concurred so that the force going out would be as large as possible.

Gerber had already shown Lucas the landing zone. They were thirty klicks from Ap Tan, and would mean a two-day march. But that would put them at the village on the evening when the VC cadre was supposed to arrive. Fetterman had a radio, and if the VC arrived earlier, he could contact the patrol, who would then increase their rate of march so they could get there in time. The distance allowed for a lot of play but wasn't so great that the patrol couldn't reach Ap Tan in a day if they had to.

Gerber stood with Tyme. He leaned close to his ear and shouted over the noise of the HUEY turbines, "Don't head straight for Ap Tan. With the size of this patrol, you're going to leave signs, but as long as they don't point directly at Ap Tan, they shouldn't give us away."

"Got it, sir," said Tyme, nodding.

"Good luck, and I'll see you in two or three days."

Tyme waved and the whole force headed for the helicopters. Once everyone was loaded, the lead ship picked up to a hover and sat back down. The dust cloud increased in size as the first aircraft began sliding forward, taking off like it was a fixed wing airplane. It came off the ground, climbed slowly, crossed over the perimeter wires, and climbed out.

The second helicopter followed the example set by lead. It made a running takeoff and climbed upward slowly to join the first. Then, in sequence, the rest of the ships took off.

Gerber stood off to the left near the base of the fire control tower and watched the whole show. He saw the flight of five finally join and turn to the east, disappearing in the distance. When they were out of sight, Gerber walked to the dispensary to check on the progress of Anh Co Duan.

Outside the dispensary, Kepler was smoking a cigarette. He was staring at the east wall as if there was something mildly interesting happening there.

He spotted Gerber and said, "Good afternoon, Captain."

"Thought you'd be inside training our agent."

"Not much training to it. She's seen the transmitter and knows how to work it. She knows that she's not supposed to do anything, search for anything, or question anybody. She's just supposed to stay home and open her eyes. I said that we would sweep through there periodically, and if she has anything, she tells us. If anything really important happens, she has the radio, but once she uses it, we pull her out of there."

"When you taking off?"

"Twenty minutes or so. Doc's going with me. I'll take ten of the Tais for the experience. Don't expect any trouble though."

"It'll be long dark before you can get back."

"Didn't think that would be a problem. We might spend the night out there. If we do, we'll give you a shout. Otherwise we should be back by midnight."

The door opened and McMillan stuck his head out. "Anytime Derek."

"How are your patients?" asked Gerber.

"Nothing drastic. Lieutenant Denton said she wouldn't mind staying an extra day or two to help out. We've cleared it with Major Acalotto. He said that there was no problem."

"Check out with me before you leave," said Gerber to Kepler. He was thinking that his force was getting a little thin. Tyme, Smith, and Washington were out with the large patrol. Fetterman was out with his. Cavanaugh was still in the hospital in Saigon. Bromhead was still in the dispensary here. Now Kepler and McMillan were going out, even if for only a couple of hours. Gerber would only have Clarke, Bocker, and Kittredge with him. A little thin, and both the medics would be gone.

"If you step into it," warned Gerber, "we won't be able to give you assistance easily. But we can evac you by helicopter if you need it."

At the south gate, twenty minutes later, Gerber watched the patrol worm their way through the concertina. Once clear of the perimeter and away from the mine field, they turned to the west, on line with the village of Cai Thoi. Kepler and a Vietnamese were on the point. Anh Co Duan was near the center of the patrol, wearing an *ao dai*. It was strange to see a woman in the countryside wearing one, but she had insisted. She was tired of black pajamas.

Just as they disappeared, Denton came up behind Gerber. "How dangerous is this?" she asked.

"This is fairly routine. We don't expect any trouble out there given how things have gone the last couple of days. That doesn't mean that they won't stumble into the enemy, but I doubt it right now."

"How can you stand the waiting?" she wanted to know.

"There isn't much choice in the matter. We have to patrol. Besides, they're all professionals, trained to do exactly what they're doing."

"You all like that word *professional*, don't you?"

Gerber turned to look at her. She held one hand over her eyes to shade them as she stared into the sun in the west, trying to catch a final glimpse of the patrol.

"I suppose we do. But it is the truth. We're not like the draftees, or even some of the volunteers.

They're in for two or three years, fulfilling a mandatory requirement. They want to survive that time with as little grief as they can. They learn what they have to to get along, and ignore the rest. When their term of service is over, they'll all get out, go to school, enter business, and tell lies about their service to their drinking buddies. But we'll still be here, learning how to be the best soldiers we can.''

Denton dropped her hand and looked at Gerber. ''Your Sergeant McMillan already gave me that speech.''

''Well, look at yourself. You don't plan to stay in the army, do you? You're going to get out and go to work in a real hospital.''

''What's wrong with that?''

''Absolutely nothing. But I'll bet you want to be the best nurse you can be. That you thought you might learn something here, in Vietnam, and that's why you're here. You're a professional, aren't you?''

''Okay, Captain,'' she said, smiling. ''I see your point.''

''Good. Now, let's go over to the team house and see about finding something to eat. You can tell me how things are shaping up in the dispensary, and I'll keep telling you how safe you are here.''

''It wasn't really my safety I was thinking of.''

Gerber looked after the now-vanished patrol and thought he understood. He was wrong, but not by much.

The first LZ was nearly due east of the camp. The helicopters dropped eastward. A hundred meters out, the door gunners opened fire, raking the treeline on the west and the empty rice paddies to the east with a couple thousand rounds of M-60 ammo. Rather than land, they hovered through, taking off again with the troops still on board. A phantom landing in case someone was watching.

They flew north and did the same thing. They didn't fire as much, but they did hover through. They turned west now, heading for the real LZ.

Once again, they approached with full suppression. There was one large clump of trees to the right front of the flight. They landed near it, and as the troops leaped out, the door guns fell silent for a moment. Lead pulled pitch and took off. As they cleared the area where the troops were, they opened fire again, until they were out of the LZ.

They had one last LZ to hit. If there were VC watching, it was hoped that there would be four reports of helicopters landing and the Viet Cong would assume that four companies were operating out there. This ploy was supposed to disguise the real LZ and the real target.

Tyme waited, crouching in the deep elephant grass until all the helicopters were gone. Then he searched for Smith. Together they organized the Vietnamese on line and assaulted the trees. No one was hiding there. There weren't even any signs that the enemy had been there recently. Smith found a broken-down tunnel, and there were the remains of a couple of overgrown bunkers.

Once the perimeter was set, Tyme, Smith, and Washington grouped with the Vietnamese officers to discuss strategy. Tyme said, "I would think we should break up into two equal units. One follows the main trail and the other flanks at four or five hundred meters. That way, if we walk into an ambush, one group will be set up to support the other. I doubt that Charlie will have anything big enough to hit us both at once.''

As the sun disappeared, Tyme took one group out of the trees. There were three Vietnamese walking point, with Tyme just behind them. There were flankers on the left but none on the right, and a rear guard of three.

Smith and Washington were with the other group. They moved out just after Tyme did and broke to the right, taking up a flanking position. The going for them was a little easier, so they made better time.

There was one rest period as the last of the sunlight faded. It was to give the men a chance to eat something and to let their eyes become accustomed to the night. Like everywhere else in that area of Vietnam, there was no artificial light. Tyme and Smith had agreed on the line of march and the compass headings before they even entered the field.

About twenty-one hundred, they moved out again. They walked slowly and carefully, but the Vietnamese weren't used to patrolling in the dark and they were making noise. Some of their equipment was rattling. They coughed. They stepped on sticks and slipped off dikes, splashing into rice paddies. Each sound was like a spike driven into Tyme, but he couldn't do a thing about it. If they slowed down, there would still be the coughing and missteps and rattling equipment.

After an hour, they stopped for another rest. Tyme looked at the stars, but they provided no answers. He walked around the perimeter and told each man to be careful. They were making too much noise. If they kept it up, everyone in South Vietnam was going to know that they were out there.

They started again, changed compass headings, moving more to the east. They passed a deserted hootch and a stand of trees. They fanned out in a dry rice paddy and then grouped together again on the other side. They crossed one shallow stream.

They entered another dry rice paddy that was bordered by a stand of trees. Halfway across it, Tyme heard a snap that sounded like it came from the trees. He halted his troops and waved them to the ground.

Just as he took a position behind a dike, there was the stuttering burst of a machine gun hidden in the treeline. All at once, a dozen other weapons opened fire, kicking up the dirt around the patrol. To their left, hidden by another rice paddy dike and in a small graveyard, a second group of VC opened fire.

Tyme had walked into an L-shaped ambush. He yelled to his people, "Open fire. Open fire."

Red-colored tracers looped out toward the enemy. Rather than using his weapon, Tyme pulled out a grenade and threw it toward the trees. It fell short, exploding in the open.

More firing came from the left. Tyme rolled to the corner of the rice paddy and looked over the top. He counted twelve enemy emplacements. He didn't know how many men were in each location. In the trees, there were another ten or twelve.

It was a stalemate. Tyme and his people couldn't move because there was too much open ground in front of them, and the enemy couldn't attack because of the open ground. He grinned to himself and aimed his shotgun. It sounded a deep-throated double boom.

Tyme was just shooting to make a little noise; the range was too great for the shotgun to be effective.

The waiting game ended abruptly. Two mortar rounds exploded near the center of the rice paddy. Screams came from some of the men and two stood up to run. They were cut down immediately.

Tyme turned and tried to spot the mortar position. He heard them fire but didn't see the flashes. They had to be well hidden in the trees. The rounds fell short of Tyme's position, showering him with dirt but no shrapnel.

On the far side of the trees, Smith had waved his patrol to the ground when he heard the first burst of fire. By searching the area, he was able to see some of the tracers bouncing around and knew where the enemy was. He watched the firefight develop so that he would know how Tyme had deployed his troops. The red tracers told Smith where the enemy was, by telling him where Tyme's fields of fire were.

Smith told his men to drop their extra equipment, their rucksacks, and check themselves for things that would rattle. He detailed five men to remain behind to guard the equipment. That included Washington, who was supposed to follow shortly to help the wounded.

Silently, the men moved through the rice paddies, to the edge of the trees. The Viet Cong entrenched there were so busy firing at Tyme's party that they neglected to post a rear guard or secure their whole area. Using knives and bayonets, Smith's men moved forward, keeping low and being quiet.

Smith was the first one to make contact with an enemy. The man was lying on the ground near the base of a tree, using a loop-shaped root to support his rifle barrel. Smith leaped onto the man's back, grabbed him under the chin, and lifted. His knife sliced through the tender flesh easily. Without a sound the VC died.

Around him, the strikers were finding the enemy. Using their rifles as clubs, their bayonets, and a couple of machetes, they closed with the Viet Cong and slaughtered them. The attack came from such an unexpected quarter that most of the enemy died before they realized that their flank had collapsed.

Smith got to his feet, moved forward and then deeper into the trees. He saw the flash of the mortar tube and the seven men standing near it. He got down, and low-crawled, keeping his eyes on the enemy's weapons. They were oblivious to everything going on around them. They wanted to annihilate the men in the paddy.

For a moment, Smith wasn't sure what to do. Then he realized that the stealth was ridiculous. The VC on the other leg of the ambush wouldn't know that he was there. He rolled to his side and pulled two grenades, straightening the ends of the pins. Then he set one down in front of him. He pulled the pin of the other, threw it, grabbed the second and did the same thing. Seconds later there were two explosions near the mortar tube.

Smith leaped up, ran forward, his rifle and bayonet in front of him. One of the VC moved and Smith bayoneted him. He quickly checked the others and discovered that the grenades had killed them.

At the far end of the treeline, he found most of his men grouped. They had security out so they wouldn't be surprised the way they had surprised the Viet Cong. Quietly, he moved them forward slightly, until they were on the left flank of the VC on the other leg of the ambush. Once there, they found what cover was available and waited.

He and Tyme had already discussed what they would do and how they would initiate it. The strange thing was, the situation was designed almost as if they had drawn it on the blackboard. Smith put two fingers in his mouth and whistled. It was a shrill, high-pitched sound that cut through the night.

In the rice paddy to the front, Tyme knew immediately what the sound meant. Smith was on the flank of the enemy, having moved through the trees. That area was secure. Tyme called to his men, forming them up so that all of them faced the ambush in front of them. Now he whistled twice, telling Smith he was ready.

The VC didn't understand what was happening. The first whistle hadn't bothered them, although it was behind them. Now that the men trapped in front of them were answering, it could only mean that the sound was a signal.

Almost as if to answer their question, firing erupted behind them. A couple fell, hit in the first volley. The others turned to meet the new threat.

Once they did so, Tyme and his people were up and running across the open ground. Smith and his men stopped shooting as suddenly as they had started, now afraid that they would be killing their friends. The Viet Cong were momentarily confused and then plunged into hand-to-hand combat with Tyme and his men.

Smith was watching the back of the area, waiting to see if any of the VC tried to run. Having routed the VC ambush was easy, but now he didn't want any of the VC getting back to tell about the size of the force they encountered. From the enemy positions in front of him, he heard a crashing, *"Boom! Boom!"* He laughed to himself and said to no one, "Old Boom-Boom has arrived again."

The two shots from Tyme seemed to signal the end of the battle. He had killed two of the enemy as they had tried to flee. Another had stood up yelling, *"Chieu hoi. Chieu hoi."* Tyme moved to the man, turned him around so that he was facing away from him. Tyme put one hand on the man's shoulder and pushed him toward Smith.

There was a final burst of firing as two VC tried to escape. They killed one of Tyme's men but were cut down before they got away.

Tyme turned his prisoner over to Smith and rushed back to his men. He got them organized and they swept through the field, checking the bodies. They found one VC who was still alive, but unlike the VC, they didn't execute him. They picked him up and carried him to the rear where Washington was treating the wounded.

Most of it was superficial. Two of Tyme's men were badly hurt thanks to the mortar fire, but Washington had stopped the bleeding and given them both morphine. They were resting.

Tyme got out the radio and called the camp. He wanted to get some helicopters out to pick up the wounded and the dead. And he wanted them to bring replacements. Since they were coming anyway, he suggested that a three-ship flight with thirty new men would be about right. That would increase the size of his force to seventy-one.

He also warned them that they had two prisoners,

one of them wounded. He figured the flight crew could guard them on the flight back. What he didn't tell them was that he would remain where he was for the rest of the night, and in the morning they would sweep through one last time to make sure that there wasn't anyone left in the field.

The radio traffic finished, he suggested that someone go back into the trees and find the mortar tube. It might have been damaged by the grenades, but if it wasn't, it could be used in the camp's defense. Free weapons, donated by the VC, were always welcome.

About the time that the firefight was erupting, Kepler and his party were leaving Cai Thoi. They had stayed for a couple of hours, talking to the villagers. McMillan used the time to hold a sick call, treating some people for injuries, for disease, and for wounds. Only a couple came by, and he did what he could for them.

Anh Co Duan, on instructions from Kepler, pretended that she didn't particularly like the Americans. The villagers noticed that she had changed in the few days she had been with the Americans, but they attached no significance to it. Once they reached the village, she went straight to the home of the family who had helped her. She didn't reappear.

As they were leaving, a young woman, the one who had a bad cut on her leg and had been given medicine by McMillan, came out of her hootch. She approached them slowly, shyly. McMillan asked if there was something else.

She responded in Vietnamese so quiet that he could barely hear. "There are some boobytraps out there."

"Where?"

"Come. I will show you."

They approached a fence and she indicated the gate. "If you open it, it will explode."

McMillan nodded his understanding. He didn't tell her that he never used gates because they were so easy to boobytrap. None of the Special Forces soldiers did. They had learned long ago by experience that you didn't open gates in hostile territory.

She walked a few hundred meters with them, pointed to places where there were other boobytraps. Finally they reached a point where she wanted to turn around and go back.

"Won't you be in danger for showing us the way?" asked McMillan.

"No. The others will not tell. They wanted me to show you because you had been kind to them. You helped them. And you healed Anh Co. They asked that I do this."

McMillan bowed slightly. "Thank you. And if any of you become ill or injured, you may always come to our camp for assistance. We have more medicine, better medicine, there."

"Thank you. I shall tell the others."

As soon as the young woman was out of sight, Kepler got on the radio to report that they had finished their mission and were on the way in. If everything went well, they expected to be there by three.

Gerber had finished eating and had gotten a cup of tepid coffee. Louise Denton was sitting next to him, finishing a glass of cool milk. Finally she said, "There is one thing that I really don't understand."

"What's that?"

"Yesterday, you and your men found fifty bodies of civilians killed by the VC, but you didn't do anything about it?"

"What could we do? We left the bodies buried and put up a marker of sorts. The Viet Cong were long gone, back to Cambodia where we can't touch them. If we had given chase, we might have been ambushed, but more likely General Crinshaw would have flown out here and relieved me on the spot."

"That's not what I meant," she said, turning so that she could look at him.

"Then I'm at a loss."

"Why didn't you get someone from the press out here. Let them print the story. Let the world, world opinion, do something about it."

Gerber smiled, but there was no humor in it. "Call in the press? You really think the press would be interested in a bunch of dead Vietnamese killed by another bunch of Vietnamese? Don't be naive."

Denton drained the glass and set it down. "What do you mean by that?"

"Just that the press would only be interested if those people had been massacred by us. Then there would be a real story. But with the Viet Cong doing it, it's old hat. It's nothing new and exciting. Besides that, it's an internal problem. Vietnamese against Vietnamese.

"I'm afraid that the people of the world couldn't care less. It has no impact on them. If our press reported it, I'm afraid that, somehow, it would come out that we were responsible for this."

"I still don't understand."

"Oh, look," snapped Gerber, "the press already has a notion of how things should be. It doesn't matter that they understand nothing about it. They assume that they are experts in everything from astrophysics to military strategies. They hear a key phrase and they know everything. The best thing for us is to have as little to do with the press as possible.''

''Oh.''

''I'm sorry, I sometimes get wound up. We have to fight for everything we get here. Supplies, information, support. Everything is a long, ongoing battle, and I don't have time to play politics with the press. There is absolutely nothing they can do for me, but they can make my life miserable.''

''And the people's right to know?'' she asked, keeping the argument going.

''Ends at the point where it becomes an invasion of my privacy and safety. Some members of the press wouldn't think twice about exposing a plan in advance because they don't believe in what we're doing. The VC read the papers. Some of the captured Viet Cong have told us that. I try to stay away from the press.''

''You seem to be very opinionated about it,'' she said, meaning no criticism.

''I don't claim to be an expert in journalism, why should I accept them as experts in military tactics?''

''It is possible that you're wrong?''

''You want just one example? If you get a chance, read a copy of the newspaper article printed just after the Custer massacre. The press was calling on Congress, wondering what the response should be. Custer and a couple of his top officers were condemned by the press. As it turned out, that battle marked the end of the Indian way of life. Never again would such a large group of Indians be able to gather. Yet the vast majority of the information printed about the Custer massacre is inaccurate. When the press didn't have answers, it made them up.''

''I think you're wrong about it.''

''All right,'' said Gerber, leaning back in his chair. ''I'll tell you what I'll do. I will alert the press, through Crinshaw's office, that we have evidence of a Viet Cong atrocity. We'll see what kind of response we get.''

''What do you expect to happen?''

''One of two things. We'll either be told that no one is available to cover it, or that since it happened a couple of days ago, it's old news. As I say, they're just not interested in that.''

On a hillside near the village of Ap Tan, Fetterman was listening to his radio. He had the earpiece attached so that only he could hear, and the insistent buzzing of the static told him that it was still working. Just before it was time for him to check in, he heard Tyme report his firefight. He listened carefully, wanting the details that Tyme would not supply on the radio. All he knew for sure was that Tyme and Smith had broken up an ambush with great skill.

To himself, Fetterman said, ''That's my boy, Boom-Boom. That's my boy.''

He had wondered how well the plan would work, but now felt that it couldn't fail. They were in place to watch for the VC propaganda cadre. They had reinforcements coming toward them slowly, who had already engaged the enemy successfully. The only way that it would work against them now was if they all were wiped out. But Fetterman knew that wouldn't happen because more strikers were available, just twenty minutes away by chopper, air support was available through Saigon, and they might even be in range of some of the big guns at the artillery base near Tay Ninh.

Fetterman broke squelch twice at midnight, telling Bocker and Gerber that he was all right. There was nothing else to report because the VC hadn't yet arrived.

Fetterman didn't know that the advance party of the VC cadre was now less than five hundred meters from Ap Tan. After the last disaster, they had decided they would check the village out before the main body arrived.

Everything was progressing as both sides had planned.

CHAPTER 10 _____

In the cold light of dawn, Fetterman was aware that something had changed in the village. It had started out as another normal day but then something subtle switched like the houselights dimming in a theater. There were no longer any young women around, there were no young men, and only a few old women who were not watching their cooking pots. He took out his binoculars and surveyed the whole scene carefully. At first there was nothing new to see, then, on the far side of Ap Tan almost directly opposite him, he saw two, then three men wearing the green uniforms of the NVA.

Fetterman reached to his right and touched Lieutenant Minh on the arm. When Minh looked at him, Fetterman surrendered the binoculars so that Minh could see. After he looked, he whispered, ''They're here?''

''Not yet. I think that is a recon party. They're checking to make sure that they're alone.''

"Should we alert the others?"

"No. Tyme will be here tonight anyway. There's nothing we can do except sit here and watch. With luck, the rest of the cadre will arrive later today."

"I will check the others and tell them that we must lay low today. I believe they will enjoy this, if they don't mind the proximity of the enemy." Minh smiled quickly and crawled off to brief the others.

Only Sergeant Krung objected with his characteristic plea to kill the communists now. Minh patiently explained that by waiting they would get to kill many more of the communists, and as a bonus, they would hurt their image of invincibility. Krung nodded his approval and said, "I keep these people quiet. No one know we here."

About ten, Gerber found Lucas sitting in the team house drinking coffee. Gerber pulled up a chair and sat down. He said, "I think we need to talk about this upcoming mission."

"What's to discuss?"

"For one thing, we can figure that it will be hot. I want to know what your pilots expect before I commit all my people to this thing. We'll need to reinforce the guys in the field."

"You got a map?"

Gerber unfolded the papers he had carried in. "This," he said, pointing to Ap Tan, "is where we're going. Now if Fetterman had his way, he'll be set up on the southeast side of the ville. Tyme will be joining him there. We'll want to put the blocking force in on the northwest side, so as Fetterman sweeps through, he'll force the enemy toward the blockers."

Lucas sipped his coffee, set the cup down, slopping some onto Tay Ninh and into Cambodia. "Well, assuming your map is good, we shouldn't have trouble with the landing zones. Ground looks like it will be solid. That close to the edge of the swamps we shouldn't be troubled with trees. It all depends on which side of that river you want to be on."

Gerber looked at Lucas's finger. He saw the tiny blue line that indicated a stream, but from the map all he could tell was that it was fairly narrow and fairly shallow.

"That will depend on Fetterman and what he says. It will depend on where the VC go."

"Ideally," said Lucas, "we'd like to land as far from the trouble as possible. But we can land on top of it, if you want."

"The plan calls for the assault to go in just as things break at the far end. If it works right, the Viet Cong will be so busy there that you'll be able to sneak in and out."

"I don't suppose that we can make a recon."

"Not today," said Gerber. "It's too risky now."

Kepler was sleeping after his night in the field. Gerber woke him and then sat down on an ammo case. Kepler had set up a cot next to one wall. Under the cot was a case of Coke and a cardboard box. An ammo case standing on its end served as a bedside table. Dirty uniforms, an extra pair of jungle boots, and a couple of olive-drab towels were on the floor.

Kepler's weapons, however, were well cared for. One stood in the corner and had obviously been cleaned just before he had gone to bed. Its magazine was sitting on the floor next to it so that he could get to both of them quickly. Under his pillow, where his hand had been, was a fully loaded Browning P-35 pistol. Three hand grenades were lined up on top of the ammo crate.

"How many agents do you have in place?"

Kepler sat up, rubbed his face, and blinked in the morning light. "Christ," he said, "my mouth tastes like the bottom of a birdcage."

"Agents?" Gerber prompted.

"We now have Anh Co Duan at home. I have two in villages close to here and am looking for others. I've only got four in place. Of course, that doesn't count the ones set up by Henderson's team."

"What's the difference?" asked Gerber.

"Not that much. It's just that I haven't had a chance to work with all the agents he established, so I don't like to claim them. Once I have an opportunity to spend some time with them all, then I'll count them."

"When will that be?"

"A month. Maybe two."

"I don't suppose you have one in Ap Tan?"

"No sir. If I had, I would have mentioned it."

"Yeah, I thought you probably would have. What's doing with our prisoner? What's his name? Thanh?"

"Yes sir. He's still giving information to me. Nothing quite as interesting as those first little tidbits."

"He ready to assist us? Go into the field with us? Maybe identify the big cheese on this thing."

Kepler stood up and stretched. He sat down and pulled on his pants. "I would think not. He might take it as a chance to bug out. Maybe not. He's thoroughly confused by all this, but I'd rather not take the chance."

"Just thought I'd ask."

"What's going on, Captain?"

"Nothing yet, but I've got a feeling that we're going to go tonight. That the propaganda cadre is going to be there and we're going to be there, ready for them."

At fourteen hundred hours, Fetterman heard a commotion in Ap Tan. He got out the binoculars and saw that the men who had been milling around on the outskirts of the village had moved to the center. They had stopped almost everyone from going into the field that day. The villagers had stayed in their hootches, waiting until the VC left.

Ten or twelve of the NVA in their green uniforms had marched to the center and begun shouting for everyone to come out. It was time to meet with the glorious representatives of the Vietnam Cong San and North Vietnam.

A few minutes later, another large group entered the village and moved among the people, talking and laughing and handing out food. They had a large sack of rice and were using a metal canteen cup to distribute it. Through the binoculars, Fetterman could see that the burlap bag had a shield painted on the front in red, white, and blue. Although it was too far away to read the label, he knew what it said because he had seen them before. "A gift from the people of the United States to the people of South Vietnam."

He pointed it all out to Minh. Then he picked up the radio and whispered, "Zulu six, Zulu six, this is one-one. It's a go. Put in at zero-zero-six-one at twenty-one. Acknowledge."

Bocker leaped to the radio and said, "Zero-zero-six-one at twenty-one." He waited for more, and when nothing came in, he ran out of the commo bunker, looking for Gerber.

Gerber saw him coming and said, "Now?"

"Twenty-one hundred. Message came in a few minutes ago."

"All right. I'll start the ball rolling here. You find Bao and tell him to get his reaction team ready. We've got a couple of hours, so let's use them the best we can."

At seventeen hundred hours, as the NVA and VC moved more men into the village, Fetterman made a final radio call. This one was meant for Tyme. Orders were that Tyme would monitor his radio at seventeen hundred. Fetterman keyed his mike and said, "Zulu base to Zulu Rover."

"Rover here."

"Seven-two-five-four-nine. Two thousand."

"Seven-two-five-four-nine. Two thousand."

"Out."

Tyme took out his map, already crisscrossed with a grid that had their own system of numbering. The message had told Tyme where to be and when to get there. He showed it to Smith and said, "We better step on it. We still have a long way to go."

McMillan stood next to the large cabinet that held most of his medicines. He was checking his field pack, replenishing his supplies, and adding extra dressings and morphine he figured he would need later.

Denton entered from the outside and saw what he was doing. "So it's tonight then."

"Yeah, but don't go spreading it around."

"Just who do you think I'm going to tell."

"Sorry. It's just my natural inclination for military secrecy showing through. Don't tell anyone what you're doing and it can't hurt you."

She had a hundred things she wanted to say but avoided them all. "What can I do to help?"

"Just be here when we get back. We'll have some wounded, I'm sure, and any extra help might save a few lives. If you can get things ready for us, it would be a big timesaver."

"That goes without saying. I'll do what I can."

McMillan looked at her, sensing that there was something more that she wanted but unsure of how to proceed. He let it go by saying, "We should be back by dawn."

As he moved to the door, she took one step forward, reaching out slightly, and then said, only, "Hey. Good luck."

Without looking at her, he said, "Thanks."

Lucas gathered the aircraft commanders and pilots near the helicopters. He had already briefed them on the locations and loads. They knew the emergency procedures, having studied them in flight school. They also knew the purpose of the mission. They understood that this was the reason they had been sent here.

Lucas finished up saying, "Our signal to land is a single red flare fired from the southeast side of Ap Tan. It won't be fired until the VC have been engaged on that side, and then we'll land on the other. With luck, we'll get out before old Charles knows that we're there."

He waited for a few minutes and then said, "Any

questions?'' When no one spoke, he said, ''Good
luck to you. Stand by at your aircraft.''

At dusk, the VC started herding the villagers to the
raised platform they had built near the chief's hootch.
They began the proceedings with a propaganda ha-
rangue that lasted nearly an hour. At the end, there
seemed to be a question-and-answer session. That
finished, they started in with the punishment for
those who had committed offenses against the great
and true government in Hanoi.

When the speeches began, Fetterman had broken
squelch twice to tell Gerber and Tyme that the meeting was starting and they should move into position
as soon as possible.

On the runway, the five helicopters sat quietly.
Gerber, having received the signal from Fetterman,
ran from the commo bunker. Lucas saw him come
out and pulled the trigger on the collective, starting
the engine. As it built power, the main rotor began to
spin, telling the others it was time to crank. They
followed suit. Within ten minutes, they were airborne.

Tyme heard the signal when he was only a thousand meters southeast of Ap Tan. He waved to Smith,
telling him to close it up, and in forty minutes they
were in position. If everything was as it should be,
Fetterman would know where they were. He would
know that the flight was off. Communication among
them was unnecessary, unless there was a foul-up.
Tyme would wait until Fetterman initiated the action,
and then move forward to Fetterman's position.

Everyone, on both sides, was now in position.
Fetterman hidden on his hillside; Tyme and Smith

below him and about a hundred meters behind him, waiting; Gerber and the reaction force airborne and circling far enough to the south that they couldn't be seen or heard, waiting to see the red flare. The VC cadre was in the center of Ap Tan telling the villagers lies. On the north, west, and southwest sides of Ap Tan were nearly two hundred NVA and VC soldiers. They were all, even though the VC didn't know it, waiting for Fetterman's red flare.

CHAPTER 11_____

It had been dark for an hour when Fetterman decided that it was time to begin the festivities. He hadn't been sure how he was going to proceed until he had watched the leader of the cadre, who, with the sadistic pleasure of the true maniac, had begun the torture of the village chief. Fetterman knew that Gerber wanted to capture as many members of the cadre as possible, but that man deserved to die.

Fetterman took his M-14 and rested it on a log in front of him. He lined up the sights so that they were high on the chest of the man he assumed to be the VC cadre leader. The man was walking around on the platform, nearly screaming at the villagers. Finally he stopped and pointed at the chief.

At that moment, Fetterman squeezed the trigger, and the weapon slammed back into his shoulder. Fetterman saw the man on the platform stagger, clutch at his chest, and drop to his knees. The sound of the shot reached them, and three or four of the cadre turned to stare.

Tyme and the men with him leaped up and ran toward Fetterman, fanning out. Tyme hit the ground next to Fetterman and said, "We're here."

"Then shoot."

There was a ragged volley from the strikers that sent everyone in the village running for cover. There was very little return fire in those first moments, only one or two shots, then more as the guard company moved into Ap Tan and started maneuvering toward Fetterman's position.

As that happened, Fetterman grabbed his red flare and fired it.

Both Gerber and Lucas saw it at the same time. Lucas, on the intercom, said, "There it is."

"Head to the LZ," said Gerber.

On the radio, Lucas said, "Come up in trail. Turning on final for the LZ. You have normal rules of engagement. Return fire for fire received, but be careful because we have people on the east side of the ville."

Gerber sat back, away from the pilots' seats, and stripped off his flight helmet. He put on his steel pot, loaded his weapon, and moved closer to the door so that he could look out.

They began their descent. Far to the east, they could see the village. They turned slightly, moving closer to it. At five hundred feet, about a klick out, the first of the enemy weapons opened fire.

Fred Chrisman keyed his mike and said, "Flight's taking light fire on the right."

Suddenly, a dozen weapons began shooting and the greet and white tracers of the VC clawed upward.

From somewhere in the darkness there was a rapid clattering of a .30-caliber machine gun. One door gunner, seeing the flash of that weapon, tried to hit it with his M-60.

The enemy became more accurate.

"Trail's taking hits."

"Flight's taking heavy fire."

"Roger," said Lucas. "Still normal rules. We don't need to tell them exactly where we are."

In front of them a platoon of VC began shooting, but the shots were wild. The VC could hear the helicopters but couldn't see them. They were shooting at the sound.

"I don't think they're very close," Ramsey said to Chrisman. But he wasn't sure because watching tracers coming toward you at night could be very deceiving.

Close to the ground now, Lucas flashed his landing light. He saw a flat plain covered with elephant grass in front of him. He flared, slowing his ship, and then leveled the skids. On the radio, he said, "Decelerate."

Ramsey hauled back on his cyclic, dropping the pitch. He lost sight of the aircraft in front of him and broke to the left, setting down in the high grass.

At that moment, a machine gun opened fire, raking the front of the helicopter, and Ramsey felt a burning in his left arm as a bullet tore through it. He squeezed the mike button on the cyclic and said, "You've got it."

Chrisman didn't respond.

Ramsey turned to look and saw that the windshield in front of Chrisman was full of holes. Chrisman was slumped in his seat, blood covering the front of his chicken plate.

"Everyone's out, sir," said the crew chief.

"Chrisman is hit. See if you can help him."

From trail came the report, "You're down with five. Fire received all over the fucking place."

"Lead's on the go." Lucas looked over his shoulder and saw Ramsey's aircraft sitting alone. A machine gun in front of it was shooting into it steadily.

Lucas's crew chief opened fire, trying to kill the enemy gunners. They switched targets, shooting at Lucas. He could feel the rounds hitting his ship, but the engine instruments remained in the green as he climbed out.

Ramsey pulled to a hover, kicked the pedals so he could maneuver around chock three—the third helicopter behind lead—which didn't move.

From trail, he heard, "You're out with four. Chock three is down in the LZ."

"I'm breaking for the hospital," said Ramsey. "I have wounded."

"I thought you were down in the LZ," said Lucas.

Trail broke in and said, "Negative. Negative. Chock three is down. He's lost his radios."

Lucas tried to raise the pilots on the radio but failed. He called for the men on the ground to check it out and report back to him.

The crew chief in Ramsey's aircraft, who had crawled out of his well, used the red handles on the back of the pilot's seat to tip it to the rear so that they could get Chrisman out. As soon as he had done this, the crew chief knew there was no hope. Chrisman had taken two bullets in the face and one in the groin. He had lost so much blood that if the bullets hadn't killed him, the loss of blood would have.

*   *   *

On the ground, Gerber saw that one of the helicopters hadn't taken off. He deployed his troops to neutralize the enemy machine guns. As they began putting out the rounds, Gerber ran to the downed ship. Both pilots were dead. The door gunner, shot through the leg, had gotten out and fallen to the ground near the aircraft. The crew chief was there trying to bandage his wound.

Gerber said, "You'll have to stay here for a while. Once we begin to move, I don't think you'll be bothered by the enemy."

The man nodded, almost as if too shocked to respond.

Gerber ran back to the edge of the LZ. Most of the enemy fire was coming from the northeast side. He could see the flashes. His men were on the ground, pinned down but shooting back. Gerber crawled along the line until he found a man with an M-79.

"Put some fire into that machine-gun position. Now."

The man got to his knees, raised his weapon, and fired one round as a burst from the machine gun caught him chest high. He fell back, dead.

The M-79 round had been perfectly placed. It silenced the machine gun.

With that Gerber was up and running, now carrying the M-79 as well as his rifle. Kittredge and Clarke were near him, and he pushed the M-79 at Clarke. Several of the Vietnamese followed. On instinct, Gerber fell to the ground as another machine gun and a group of AKs began to take the LZ under fire.

Gerber used his M-14 with little effect. He couldn't

see the enemy, but he could hear shouts in Vietnamese. Once he saw a fleeting shadow near a group of trees but didn't have the chance to shoot. He used one grenade, then another.

Clarke did the same with the M-79. As the grenades exploded, he leaped to his feet, rushing up the hill at the VC. He didn't realize that he was screaming at them.

The whole line was now advancing, firing from their hips, running toward the enemy. A couple fell, but the charge seemed to pick up a momentum of its own, carrying everyone with it. The shooting increased in volume. Over it, nearly everyone was shouting and cursing.

They reached the front of the VC line and for a moment the fighting was hand to hand. Gerber shot one of the enemy who seemed to rise out of the ground before him. He then spun to the right, saw another VC, and hit him with a vertical butt stroke.

The shooting tapered off as the two forces became mixed. The sound was now of grunting men, fighting with knives and bayonets. But the attack had been too fierce and almost too surprising. In panic, some of the VC began to flee.

There was a shrill whistle from behind the enemy. It came once and then twice, almost as if it was a rallying call. Now the Viet Cong began to move toward it, breaking contact with Gerber and his men. As they did so, they opened fire again, forcing the men with Gerber to take cover.

Far to the rear, suddenly silhouetted against the sky, Gerber saw a lone man waving to his troops. He was shouting instructions and pointing, trying to force his men down the other side of the hill to the village. Gerber fired half a dozen shots but the man wasn't hit. Too late, Gerber realized that he was trying to get the Viet Cong to fall back into the village where they could reinforce the enemy.

As the shooting on the hill faded, Clarke ran up. "We've taken about fifteen casualties."

"Have doc look at them. Get the rest organized here and prepare to move into the ville. We've got to move to support Fetterman or he's going to be in trouble."

"Tyme's on his side."

"But they're still outnumbered. We've got to hit their flank and break them up."

From his position, Fetterman could see the tracers being fired at the helicopters. He whispered to Tyme, "They're really catching it there." Then he was too busy with the fight on his end to worry about it.

Tyme had spread his people out along the top of the ridge. The main force was with him. A couple of squads were covering the right flank, where they thought the major counterattack might come from. They didn't really expect a frontal assault, but with the VC you could never tell.

At first, as they had opened fire, there had been a number of figures scurrying around inside the village, but as the thatch of the roofs began to burst into flame and the interior of Ap Tan became bright, that stopped. The return fire came in sporadic ripples, as if no one down there knew what to do.

As the fighting began at the other side of the village, triggered by Gerber and the helicopters,

Fetterman and Tyme ordered an advance. They started it with a volley of rifle shots and hand grenades. When the final one exploded, obscuring the village behind it in dust and smoke, they rushed forward.

Before the VC there knew what hit them, Fetterman and a group of strikers had captured a hootch on the edge. Fetterman had tossed a single grenade in the door, waited for the explosion, and dived in. He found a body holding a shrapnel-riddled AK-47. Fetterman took the weapon and ran back out.

Tyme and three strikers were pinned down by a machine gun. Each time one of them looked up, the machine gunner fired. Tyme used his shotgun, spraying the area with double-ought buck, but missed the machine gunner. He kept shooting.

Twenty meters away, Smith was having a similar problem with three or four men barricaded in a hootch. They had AK-47s and knew enough to rotate the firing so that they didn't all run out of ammo at the same moment. Grenades either fell short or exploded harmlessly at the side of the hootch. Smith kept firing single-shot at the windows, trying to pick off one of the men.

On the north end of the line, more than a dozen VC held the rest of the strikers in check. They were throwing out rounds just as fast as they could. Occasionally they threw Chinese grenades that sometimes exploded but did little damage.

In fact, the whole line had stopped, taking cover at the very edge of the settlement. Fetterman ran back to the hootch he had taken, went in, and found the back wall. He felt along it, looking for holes or windows, but found none. He stepped back and, holding his

rifle at hip level, opened fire on full auto. The heavy
M-14 bullets smashed through the flimsy mud, creating a peephole for him. He ran to it and looked out.
Far to the right, he could see one man standing
behind the VC, urging them forward.

To himself, Fetterman said, "I've seen that guy
before. I know I have."

There was enough light from the burning hootches
to allow Fetterman to use his sights. He lined them
up carefully and began to squeeze the trigger, but
before the weapon fired, the man dropped to one
knee and then crawled out of sight.

Fetterman opened fire anyway, throwing rounds in
the general direction of the man. He was answered
by a volley that slammed into the walls of the hootch,
splattering him with dirt and debris. Fetterman dropped
flat.

With the point of concentration of the fire shifted,
the men on the north side of the village jumped up.
Lieutenant Minh led them forward, overrunning a
couple of the VC positions. For a few minutes the
fighting was hand to hand. Minh was knocked to the
ground by a rifle butt to his shoulder but rolled clear
of the bayonet. He kicked at the feet of the enemy
soldier, tripping him. When the man fell, Minh shot
him in the head.

One of the strikers saw Minh go down and thought
he had been killed. He rushed forward to check the
lieutenant, but a VC soldier stood up and bayoneted
him. The striker fell to his knees as the Viet Cong
jerked the bayonet free. Minh shot that man too.

There were a couple more shots but the enemy
position had been captured. Minh got to his feet,

found the bodies of two more of the strikers, and then had the living fall back about ten yards to the protection of a mud wall.

Meanwhile, Smith had been crawling toward the hootch where the enemy was. He had given up trying to shoot them because they were being too careful. He had found a depression running to the west, almost right at the hootch, and had dropped into it. All he could see was the very top of the hootch and figured that the enemy couldn't see him.

He came to the end of it and found that he was under one of the firing ports. Hoping that the Viet Cong wouldn't be able to see him, Smith crawled out of the depression and was next to the wall of the hootch. He eased himself along it until he could see the door. With one hand, he reached for a grenade, pulled the pin, and tossed it at the door. It hit the wall and rolled, exploding in front of the hootch. Shrapnel hit the wall near him and he grinned. "Blow yourself up, dummy."

Again he tried it and this time the grenade hit the edge of the door but rolled inside the hootch. Smith got to his hands and knees after the grenade exploded and threw himself through the door. He rolled to his right, hit the wall, and came up firing at a shadow. A second later he saw that it was only a shadow. His own.

Two of the VC were dead, but the third was only stunned. Smith jerked his weapon away from him and covered him as a couple of his strikers came in. Smith said, "You keep him here and watch him."

With the support on the right and left gone and with Fetterman firing at them with apparent impunity, the machine gunners who had pinned Tyme down picked up their weapon and ran to the north. They found a group of NVA deployed around three hootches. They had set up interlocking fields of fire. Each position could easily support each of the others.

Tyme fired a couple of shots at the fleeing enemy. One fell, dropping the machine gun. Another stopped, hesitated as if he wanted to grab the gun, but Tyme fired again and the man ran. Tyme got to his feet and headed for the hootch where Fetterman was still taking potshots at the fleeing enemy.

On the right, Minh was also shooting, putting a high volume of fire into the Viet Cong strong point. There were grenade blasts, but neither side could advance.

Gerber and his men had reached the very edge of Ap Tan and halted for a moment. Then they swung to the south, searching for the remnants of the VC guard company. They could hear the firefight going on between Fetterman and the VC on the east side of the village. Gerber hoped to come up behind some of the enemy, surprise them, and force them to either surrender or flee.

Firing around them had tapered off to an occasional sniper round. Most of these were greeted with grenades and then a couple of people to make sure that the sniper was dead.

They advanced slowly. Gerber and Clarke were on the point, more or less. They were listening and searching, but they couldn't see anything. Gerber knew that the enemy had to be around somewhere.

Clarke eased toward Gerber. He wanted to take

part of the people farther to the south so that they could come up behind anyone who engaged Gerber. Before he could speak, a single shot rang out and Clarke dropped immediately.

Gerber crouched near him, looking to the front and feeling for Clarke's throat. He said, "Miles? Miles? Are you okay?" Then he looked down, found the throat, and felt for a pulse. There was none.

Sighing, Gerber got to his feet and took three running steps to the front. He dived to the ground and waited, but the sniper apparently felt that he had done his job and faded into the night.

There was a brief flurry of firing then, returned by the strikers. They tossed a few grenades. Then, in support of them, the two squads left by Fetterman as flank security started shooting from the other side, and the VC caught in the crossfire either died or surrendered.

Gerber waved a couple of his strikers to him, and together they advanced toward the VC. Gerber kept his eyes on the hands of the enemy, waiting for them to try something. But they didn't move. The strikers picked up the weapons, and then two of them, as guards, forced the enemy to walk to the LZ.

With that the majority of the resistance in the village collapsed. Gerber joined the flank squad and then moved to the north. He found Fetterman and Tyme, who were crouched behind a hootch. There were only a few shots being fired.

"What's the situation here?" asked Gerber.

"We have a group of them cornered in three or four hootches over there."

"Well, let's get them. It shouldn't be hard now."

"They're very well trained, Captain," said Fetterman. "They've deployed themselves almost perfectly."

"Are you suggesting that we can't take them?"

"Of course not. I was merely suggesting that it might take a little time to do it right."

Gerber turned and looked at the enemy position. There were no obvious weaknesses to exploit. He glanced to the right, saw that Minh was setting up his machine guns and bringing them to bear on the enemy-held hootches. He began to rake them with a heavy fire.

On the left, Krung was checking the bodies of the dead enemy and had several of his men out as pickets. They were shooting into the hootches but with no real concentration of fire. They were just shooting to be shooting.

"Let's get this over with," said Gerber. "Justin, get some of the M-79s up here. I'll want a barrage of them, mingled with hand grenades. Then we'll advance."

"Captain, the firing from there is tapering. I think they may be bugging out."

"Then we'd better hurry."

Tyme ran off, crouched. He returned a couple of minutes later with three grenadiers. Gerber set them where he wanted, gave them instructions, and then told everyone with him to take one hand grenade, and on his command they would all throw them. He told the grenadiers to use willy pete—white phosphorus— for illumination, if they had it.

With that ready, Gerber yelled "Fire!"

The grenades arched out and the M-79s popped. There was a series of explosions. Gerber jumped up and called, "Let's go."

There was a shout behind him, and most of the men advanced on the hootches. There was no return fire. Gerber leaped over one of the low fences surrounding a hootch and crouched on one knee. The others followed him. Fetterman dived into one of the hootches and emerged quickly. Tyme took another one.

"They're gone, Captain," said Fetterman.

Three Viet Cong, dressed in green pajamas, emerged from the hootch, followed by Tyme, who said, "There's a couple of bodies in here with weapons."

Fetterman walked around the prisoners, being careful not to get between them and Tyme. Inside, he checked the bodies one last time and picked up the weapons. He searched for a moment and found a stash of papers. He collected those too.

Outside again, he said, "Let's get these people and papers over to Kepler." He directed a couple of the strikers to take charge and head to the LZ.

"Lieutenant Minh," called Gerber. "Over here."

"What can I do for you, old boy?"

"You didn't see them getting out?"

"No. We kept up a sustained fire to hold them down, but we didn't see them evacuating."

"Fetterman, you check out the hootches for tunnels and bunkers, and let's be careful. We've done too well to lose a bunch of people for nothing."

Carefully, Fetterman entered the center hootch. Covered by Kepler and two strikers, he probed the floor and sides of the hootch but found nothing other than the normal things in a villager's dwelling.

It was the same in the others. No hidden tunnels or bunkers. It was as if the war had not touched this area for so long that the people no longer felt they needed these things. If it had been a Viet Cong village, there should have been a tunnel for a quick getaway.

"Okay then," said Gerber, "get some security established. I'll want a sweep-through here. Put the villagers into one area but see that they get food and medicine, if they need it. Tony, you get a count on wounded and we'll call for evac for them. We may only have three helicopters.

"Justin," Gerber continued heavily, "I think Sergeant Clarke is dead. His body is about due south of here, near the place where your flankers were. Let's recover him.

"Lieutenant Minh, let's check the bodies of the VC. We don't want any of them behind us."

"What about the ones who escaped?"

"Let them go. It will be impossible to find them in the dark without taking a bunch of casualties. Right now we have a major victory over them and a few prisoners. I think we've broken the usefulness of the propaganda cadre."

Fetterman interrupted. "Captain, I saw him again."

"Who?"

"That man I told you about after the raid on the VC base. The one who had organized his troops so well. Kepler said that he might be a Chinese adviser."

"I saw him too," said Gerber. "So?"

"Let me have a patrol. Ten guys and Boom-Boom. We'll get the bastard."

For a moment, Gerber considered it and then said, "No. We've got to stay here and clean this up. I wouldn't be able to support you out there. You wouldn't be able to track him in the dark, and you might walk into an ambush. I'm sorry, but no."

"Captain, we can take him."

"No. Drop it. We've got too much to do here. I've lost enough of my team for one night."

McMillan found Gerber and said, "We've got four people that need to be evacced now. I think we can save them if we can get them to the camp. With Denton there, we can do them enough good so they'll survive the flight to Saigon."

To Fetterman, Gerber said, "Get on the horn and get a chopper in here. I want you to secure the LZ and arrange that."

Fetterman knew that he wasn't going to convince Gerber that they should try to find the Chinese officer. He said, "Yes sir."

"Doc, you and Washington take care of our people first, but if any of the villagers need help, you give it. Okay."

"Yes sir."

"Let's start getting this organized. I want to be out of here by daylight. Derek, you want to see what you can learn from the villagers, and maybe talk to the prisoners. The cadre probably left behind some papers."

"From what I've seen," said Kepler, "I think most of the cadre is dead. As a propaganda tool, they're through."

"Let's learn what we can. Get a head count of our people and make sure we can account for them all. There's plenty to do before we can get out of here."

Northwest of Ap Tan, the Chinese officer with seven men and the leader of the propaganda cadre were holed up in a stand of trees, watching the trail behind them. They were prepared to ambush anyone following them. When there was no evidence of pursuit, they moved out, but not toward Cambodia, figuring that the Americans would assume that. Instead they turned to the southwest, almost running toward Cai Thoi. It was the location of their last successful rally, and they were reasonably sure they would receive some help there.

CHAPTER 12 _____

Gerber was crouched near the wreckage of one of
the helicopters. The front end had been laced with
automatic weapons fire. The two pilots, killed at that
moment, still sat strapped into their seats. Their blood
had splattered the instrument panel, the windshield,
and the pedestal. Even if they hadn't been killed, it
was doubtful that they could have taken off. They
had crashed onto a pointed stump that had been
hidden in the deep elephant grass. It was jammed
into the helicopter near the hellhole and had ruptured
one of the fuel cells.

The crew chief still held the head of the dead door
gunner. He had been hit once in the leg, but as the
strikers had advanced toward the hill, a wild second
shot had hit him in the head. The crew chief refused
to move.

Near Gerber were most of the wounded. Seven
men, who had been seriously injured, had already
been taken out. McMillan had gone with them, hop-

ing to save their lives at the camp. Washington was still working on a series of minor wounds, burns, breaks, and cuts.

Fetterman sat with a map spread out in front of him, trying to read it in the dim light cast by his flashlight. He measured the distances and said, "If we insert here, just south of the parrot's beak, we might be able to get that Chinese bastard."

"Tony, you don't even know if he is Chinese. Besides, we have sent him home with his tail between his legs. Let it go."

"Captain, this is the second, maybe third time our paths have crossed. Once might be happenstance, twice might be coincidence, but three times is enemy action. He's out there laying for us. I'd like to get him before he springs something really wild."

"What are you talking about?"

"I think this is also the guy from Nhu Ky."*

Gerber shook his head. "Not likely, Tony. Look, forget it. The only thing we want now is to confirm that we nailed that propaganda cadre." Gerber turned his attention to Kepler. "What have you found out?"

"The people are a little frightened of us. After all, we did just charge into their village. However, from what I've been able to piece together, we did hit the propaganda cadre that had been in Cai Thoi. I think some of them got away, but I do know that two are dead. The one Fetterman shot, a sort of leader in training, and one other. I think we have three captured with the VC who surrendered, but I don't have ID on them yet. Not confirmed ID, but I think they are the ones in the green pajamas."

*See The Scorpion Squad #2—The Nhu Ky Sting

"I want you to take them and a couple of other high-ranking prisoners back to camp on the next chopper. Show them to Thanh if you have to, but get me something. Also, call Saigon and tell them what we have. Tell them that we think we've broken up this unit and would like to know where they've been and what they've been taught."

"Yes sir."

Minh came up then and said, "We've got the area secure, old boy. I have my chaps set around as perimeter guard."

Then, almost as if to make a liar out of him, a shot was fired. It struck the helicopter high, near Gerber's head. They all dived, with Gerber saying, "Anyone see where that came from?"

Kepler whispered, "To our two o'clock, about two hundred meters."

"I'll get a squad and go for him," said Minh by way of apology.

Fetterman had rolled away and had taken an M-79 away from one of the grenadiers. He fired a round of willy pete, which exploded into flames.

"That where you saw him?" asked Fetterman.

"Close enough."

Minh started to get up. "I'll take my men up there and see what we can find."

Ten minutes later, a helicopter landed and took no fire. Gerber stepped up on the skid so that he could talk to the pilot, Captain Lucas.

"How many you got flying?"

"Just the three. Can put up number four in a real bind, but I'm short a pilot."

"Okay, take Kepler and some of his prisoners to camp and then come back here with all three. We'll evac the rest of the wounded and some of the others. How long can you remain flying?"

"We topped off on the last run. Should have about two hours."

"Like to get nearly everyone ferried back home tonight. I'll leave a twenty-man patrol out here to make a recon in the morning."

"No problem. Be back here in a few minutes with the rest of my people."

At the camp, McMillan and Denton worked through the night trying to save lives. McMillan requested two medivac flights for some of the seriously wounded. By dawn, everyone who needed special treatment was gone and the wounded who remained were resting.

McMillan looked at Denton. She was wearing a blood-spattered white smock. Her hair was a tangled mess and there were dark smudges under her eyes from lack of sleep. He uncorked a bottle of Beam's and said, "You want a a drink."

"Nah." She smiled. "I don't want one. I need one. A big one, if you can manage it."

"Listen, I just want to thank you for your help one last time. You probably saved a couple of these boys tonight."

"It was nothing."

"Sure it was. I want you to know how much I appreciate your being here. I couldn't have done it alone. I wanted to say that before you leave today."

She set her glass down and asked, "I leave today?"

"I'm afraid so. Your Major Acalotto has more or less demanded it and Captain Gerber had to go along."

She glanced back to the empty cot in the storage room and said, "Then let me say good-bye properly."

"I thought you'd never ask."

Kepler, with a dozen strikers acting as guards, was attempting to interrogate his prisoners. He had the three he suspected of being the cadre with him, trying to get them to talk. He knew that he would have no success because he didn't have the time to do it properly. He was just going through the motions and hoping that one of them would let something drop by accident.

About dawn, Bocker knocked on the door to catch his attention and then waved him outside. When they were alone, he said, "Just got a message in from Cai Thoi. Your friend there has broken radio silence to let us know that the man who leads the cadre is hiding in the village. Him and six or seven others."

"You told the captain?"

"He's still in the field."

"You better get him on the radio and tell him to get in here. Who's back?"

"Kittredge. So's McMillan."

"Tell Kittredge to find us about twenty strikers and have them prepare for a patrol. I don't know if the captain will want to do it that way but let's be ready. And tell him to bring in Tony because he'll want to get those guys."

An hour later, Gerber sat in a chair, feeling as if he was ready to collapse. Fetterman was leaning against the wall, his eyes closed. Tyme was sitting on the floor, staring down the barrel of his shotgun, having just run a cleaning cloth through it.

"Are you sure they'll still be there?"

"No sir, I'm not. But look at this logically. They'll think they're safe because we can't possibly know where they are. I figure they'll want to lay low for the day, resting, and head back to Cambodia tonight."

"There's seven of them "

"Six or seven."

Fetterman opened his eyes and said, "I'll bet that Chinese sonofabitch is with them. Let's go after them, Captain. You said if we found a trail in the morning, we could."

"I don't think those were my exact words, Master Sergeant"—Gerber smiled—"but I understand your meaning."

"Besides," said Fetterman, "you wanted to capture the leader of the cadre and you don't have him yet."

"I don't have to be reminded of that," replied Gerber sourly. "It would be an opportunity to set some things straight though. Okay, we'll do it."

"I'll go too," said Tyme.

"Of course you will, Boom-Boom," said Fetterman.

Gerber, thinking out loud, said, "We'll have Lucas put us down near Cai Thoi and walk in. He can put a blocking force between the ville and the border. Give us about a four-to-one advantage. Go in about three so we'll have several hours of daylight left."

Fetterman stood up straight. "I'll go find Lieutenant Minh and tell him we'll need a team from him."

"You organize that. Everyone take extra ammo and enough food for one meal. We'll plan to be out of there by nineteen hundred. One way or the other."

*   *   *

Lucas found Ramsey sitting in the cargo compartment of one of the helicopters, looking over the revetment at the front of the aircraft where Chrisman had died. Periodically, he would start to count the bullet holes on the right side of the windshield but always lost track somewhere around twenty or thirty.

"How's the arm?" asked Lucas.

"It'll be fine. A little stiff. Bullet just grazed me and the doc here fixed it."

"You up to another flight?"

Ramsey turned to look at, but didn't focus on Lucas. "Why?"

"Finish what we started last night. Gerber said they have information that the VC have holed up in a village near here."

"What's the point?"

"Listen, Charles, I understand how you feel. You lost one good friend last night, but I lost four. I've had to call back to our base and explain to the company commander how I managed to lose such a large portion of the flight. I've—"

"Listen to yourself," flared Ramsey. "You don't care about the people who died. They're just an inconvenience for you. You have to explain how they got killed. Next you're going to tell me that the army lost some valuable men because the army had spent so much money training them. Christ, man, they are dead and we can't tell them we're sorry about that. We'll never see them again."

Lucas rubbed his face. "I'm sorry. I guess since we're in a war, we should all be able to handle this kind of situation. No one tells you what to say to someone who has lost a friend. Should I say it was quick and merciful? Should I say that you're lucky because Fred didn't die in your arms? I don't know what to say to you. I'm sorry about it and I wish that I could fix it, but I can't. There's nothing I can do except tell you that it does no good to sit here.''

"I know that. It just seems that we should do something more. Men died last night and here we are, a couple of hours later, about to go on as if nothing happened.''

"No, not as if nothing happened. We'll remember what happened, and we have a chance to even the score that much more. Last night, according to Gerber, we killed or captured over a hundred of the enemy. Now we can get the leadership. You want to go or not?''

For a long moment, Ramsey sat staring at the bullet-riddled helicopter. Without looking away from it, he said, "Yeah. Yeah, I'll go.''

Outside the dispensary, the bodies of the strikers killed in the fight were laid out one next to the other and wrapped in green body bags. Inside, the body of Sergeant Clarke, wrapped in its body bag, waited for the aircraft that would take it to Saigon for shipment home. The one thing that Saigon managed to do with great efficiency was to get the bodies home. It was bad for morale to have the dead lying around too long.

Gerber entered the dispensary, walked straight to the cot where Clarke lay, and stared down silently for a minute or more, his head bowed. It was his salute to a fallen comrade. Then he set a clean, green beret on Clarke's chest and whispered, "It's the best I can do for you, friend.''

Without a word to either McMillan or Denton, he left.

Denton watched the whole process and then said, "He must be a good man to work for. He cares for his people."

"That he does."

Denton's equipment, the little she had brought, was sitting on the floor near the door. She was scheduled to leave on the plane that would take out the bodies. When Gerber left, she took McMillan's hand. "Write to me once in a while."

"I'll do better than that," said McMillan. "I'll come and visit you once in a while. If you like."

"That would be nice."

At fifteen hundred, while the remains of the flight cranked up on the runway, Gerber told Smith, "You don't have to do a thing. Just find a good place for an ambush on the west side of Cai Thoi. You'll be put in about two klicks west and will have to move to within a klick."

"I'll be ready in less than an hour."

"We're going to land about sixteen hundred to the southeast and sweep to the north and west, hoping to force the VC out toward you."

"Got it, Captain. See you in a couple of hours."

Smith trotted off toward the flight line, and Gerber watched as the helicopters lifted and then disappeared. Under his breath he said, "Good luck, Sully."

Thirty minutes after Smith took off, a plane landed to pick up the bodies and to fly Louise Denton back to Nha Trang. She stood at the side of the runway near the commo bunker.

Gerber found her there. He said, "You remember what we talked about?"

"You mean the newspapers and reporting the atrocity at Tuy Dong?"

"Well, I called Crinshaw earlier to report our actions of the last few days and told him what we found at Tuy Dong. I suggested that he pass it along to his friends in the press."

"And," she prompted.

"And some of them were mildly interested in talking about the mission last night, although the results weren't all that impressive. But none of them wanted to fly out here for the story of the atrocities. One of them said that there had already been too many stories like that and the people had become immune to them. Just didn't care."

"You're not serious?"

Gerber shook his head. "I'm afraid that I am. I told you. No one cares."

To the north they heard the engines of the Caribou crank up. She looked toward it and said, "There's my plane."

Gerber reached out to shake her hand. "Thank you for caring, Lieutenant, and for all your work here."

"It was nothing," she said modestly.

"It was something. It was a lot more than that."

A little before sixteen hundred, the three helicopters took off again, holding twenty-one men. Gerber was on the lead ship, Fetterman on the second, and Tyme on the third. They had talked about the sweep for forty minutes and understood exactly what they needed to do.

They landed only fifty meters from Cai Thoi in a

huge open field. Even before the aircraft had touched down, the men were leaping to the ground, dropping from the skids. When they all were unloaded, they spread out, on line, and began a rapid walk toward the village, avoiding the paths and dikes. In seconds they were at the edge of Cai Thoi, looking at the numerous people who watched them curiously.

Now, following the plan, Tyme and his group of six ran around the east end, taking a place at the northernmost corner. Fetterman moved after him, putting his men at the east side, and Gerber remained in place on the southeast. All three teams could easily see one another. On a signal from Gerber, they advanced.

Each squad checked out the hootches directly in front of them, and each signaled the other that nothing had been found. They moved slowly toward the center of Cai Thoi.

Gerber came around the corner of a hootch, caught a flash of light, and jumped back as a shot was fired. The round hit the mud wall near his chest.

Fetterman saw the muzzle flash and dropped to one knee, cranking out three rounds. That was answered from another direction by a burst from an AK.

"Well, shit," said Fetterman, only mildly irritated.

From his position near the northernmost hootch, Tyme saw one of the enemy soldiers plainly. He opened fire with his shotgun, the single boom overpowering everything else. The VC was shoved to the side.

With that, the men in Tyme's squad ran to a low fence of bush, branches, and mud. Carefully they looked around, but there was no longer any movement.

At the sound of the first shot, the villagers had scattered, some of them fleeing out of Cai Thoi to the south. A couple ran toward Tyme, but he could see that they carried no weapons and he let them go.

Single shots were still coming from a hootch about fifty meters away. Gerber could see the man's location, but never really saw him. Standard procedure would be to use grenades, but there were too many civilians around. Gerber had the men in his squad open fire, trying to kill the man, but wouldn't allow them to hose down the whole area.

Fetterman was up and running. He rolled next to a wheel of an oxcart and yelled, "Tell them to cease fire."

Fetterman expected the man to begin shooting again, but he didn't. Behind the hootch, Fetterman saw movement ad crawled forward, trying to see better. A single shot kicked up dirt near him.

Tyme saw that. He leaped the fence, hit the corner of a hootch for cover, and then dropped to one knee. He fired his shotgun, but without effect.

Two men followed him. He pointed to the rear, telling them to go around the hootch the other way. Just as they stepped into the open, they were shot at. One of them was hit and fell. The other jumped back, taking cover behind the hootch.

The wounded man lay still, but the VC kept shooting at him, trying to make sure that he was dead. Tyme ran along the side of the hootch, fired his weapon, and reached out for the wounded man. Firing increased in volume, but Tyme grabbed the left arm of the man and dragged him to cover. He wasn't badly hurt.

"Did you see the man?" asked Tyme.

"He was near the tree by the hootch."

Tyme got down to his stomach and peeked around the corner of the hootch but couldn't see anything. He fired once, but didn't draw anything in return. It seemed that the man who had been there had run away.

Waving his squad forward, Tyme ran around the corner and straight for the tree. He hit it with his back and looked around it. On the ground he found a dozen empty shell casings.

Fetterman, seeing this, ran to the hootch where another man had been hidden. He entered it and found it empty. On the dirt floor near the rear wall was a bamboo mat. Fetterman kicked it out of the way and discovered a hole leading down and out. For a moment he debated and then yelled the only Vietnamese that he knew, *"Chieu hoi."*

There was no answer. He was going to toss a grenade down the hole, into the tunnel, but was afraid that civilians would be in there. And if they were, the VC would force them to the front so that they would absorb the shrapnel.

Grinning, Fetterman took a grenade and unscrewed the fuse. He then tossed the useless weapon into the hole and leaped back, waiting. Three people scrambled out. Two women and a young boy. A moment later a fourth head slowly appeared. Fetterman fired once, the bullet hitting about four inches to the right of the head.

"Chieu hoi. Chieu hoi," the man yelled.

"Come on out of there, Charlie."

Outside, Gerber realized that the sniping was intended just to slow them down. He got up and ran along the southern edge of the village, trying to flank the VC. He saw one man moving and fired at him. The man fell, dropping his AK-47, but then tried to crawl into the closest hootch. Gerber put a round into the ground near him and the man raised his hands.

Fetterman got his men to their feet and headed them toward the center of the village. They passed Tyme's squad and when they were about even with Gerber, more shooting erupted. This time it was from the northwest corner of the village.

Tyme immediately responded with a fusillade from his squad. He ran forward, diving for cover in a ditch near the front of a hootch.

Having turned his prisoner over to one of the Vietnamese strikers, Gerber ran toward the firing. He found protection behind the corner of a mud hootch. He saw a couple of muzzle flashes and fired at them.

Fetterman joined him. They fanned the two squads out so that they held a semicircular line stretching from the northern edge of the village, through the center, then to the western side. One by one, covering each other, they tightened the circle, forcing the VC back into a single hootch that stood by itself on the northwest corner of Cai Thoi.

At first, the VC were firing rapidly. But then the shooting tapered off until the incoming was only single-shot. Gerber ran to the west, around the end of his squad. The area was open ground with no cover at all. He had been afraid that the VC would escape through tunnels, but now he could see the rear of the hootch. There was nowhere they could go.

Tyme had one of the Vietnamese strikers call to the barricaded VC, telling them that they would be well treated if they surrendered. They would not be killed.

He was answered by a rifle shot.

Again, they all opened fire. Gerber watched the back of the hootch, but still there was no evidence of an escape attempt.

Using fire and maneuver, Fetterman had his squad advanced until they were only twenty meters from the hootch. Fetterman tossed one grenade toward it so that it would land near the door. After it exploded, he yelled for them to surrender or they would all die. A Vietnamese striker repeated the words in Vietnamese.

Gerber's squad fired a volley at the hootch as if to show them that they were nearly surrounded and badly outnumbered. Only after they repeated the volley were there shouts from inside. A weapon flew out the door, and then another. Two men followed them.

One of Tyme's men told them to come forward and then lie down on the ground. He asked if there were any others inside. The men said there were not.

Three strikers from Tyme's squad ran to the side of the hootch. They approached the front and one of them dived through the door. He was met with a short burst from an automatic weapon. The second man pulled a grenade and tossed it through the door.

Fetterman jumped up and yelled, ''No!''

There was a blast from inside the hootch. Fetterman dived through the door, rolled once and came up on a knee. On one side of him was a dead striker and on the other, dressed in a clean, green uniform, was the leader of the propaganda cadre.

Quickly, Fetterman searched the hootch. There was no escape tunnel, no hidden bunker, no hiding places. Fetterman tossed around the furnishings, the bamboo mats, the worn clothing, searching, but the Chinese officer was gone. Fetterman didn't know if he had been in the hootch or not, but suspected that he had been in the village. Somehow, the man had eluded them again.

Maybe that was why the VC had put up the standing fight they had. To give the Chinese man time to get away. Fetterman's only hope now was that he would be caught by Smith's platoon west of Cai Thoi, but somehow he thought that the man wouldn't fall into that trap.

Whoever he was, Fetterman realized that he was a worthy opponent, and he was sure that they would cross paths again. To the empty hootch, Fetterman said, "You can count on it."

CHAPTER 13 ⸻⸻⸻⸻⸻⸻⸻

The surviving members of the flight crews and the majority of the Special Forces soldiers were in the team house for a last meeting. Captain Lucas sat behind a long table in the front with Captain Gerber. On the table in front of them was a huge pile of documents, captured weapons, uniforms, and North Vietnamese money.

In front of each man was one cold beer. Gerber had told Colonel Bates what he wanted. Ice was a commodity that was hard to find in South Vietnam, but Bates had located enough to nearly freeze two cases of beer. As each man entered the briefing, Gerber handed him one can as a reward, small though it was.

That finished, he moved back to the front and sat down next to Lucas, letting the men drink for a moment. Finally, he said, "Before you all leave here, I think it only fair to try to tell you exactly what we have accomplished. To let you know how important these missions really were. Without your support here, we never would have made it happen.''

Gerber took a long pull at his beer. "First, the Viet Cong propaganda cadre, by their presence, was undermining everything we did. We might be able to establish a base in the middle of their territory, but if that was all we could do, the VC still ruled. If they could roam the countryside at will, it proved that we were weak. That we were powerless to stop them.

''With your help, we were able to destroy that. We captured the majority of the cadre on their home ground. We destroyed their company of guards. Now, maybe that will yield additional information, and maybe it won't. But the point is, we defeated them again.

''We were able to do that because you were here. We could never have stopped that meeting at Tuy Dong if it hadn't been for the airlift. We just couldn't have gotten there in time. And we destroyed them at Ap Tan because we could put a large mobile force in there.''

Gerber stopped talking for a moment, wondering if they really wanted to hear this. Then he remembered something that he had overheard. One of the pilots telling another that he was glad to be part of the mission because he felt they were actually doing something that might have an impact on the war.

He continued. ''Second, we showed the VC that we could get anywhere they could, and we could do it faster. The VC might pick the battleground, but we would select the time. We would go to them and engage them at will.

''We showed the Viet Cong that they aren't safe anywhere around here. Anywhere Charlie goes, we can go. We showed him the power of aviation, and maybe showed him that he can't win, even when he has us outnumbered.''

Gerber stood and held his beer high. ''I really don't know how to tell you all that you've done for us. We will be sorry to lose you. Your dedication and professionalism is a tribute to you, and a credit to the United States Army.''

Now Gerber realized that he was saying all the things that he always hated to hear others say. It had all been said so many times before that it had become trite and almost insincere. The men in the room knew they had done a good job. His little speech told them how much they had done to the VC. It was time to end this and drink the beer.

''Gentlemen, thank you. Here's to your health.'' Gerber finished his beer in one long gulp and then tossed the empty can at the open door. The other members of the team followed suit, standing to finish the toast.

''One last thing,'' said Gerber. ''When you hold the memorial service for the men who died, please let us know. Even if we all can't get there, we would all like to attend. As final tribute to those men.''

Then Gerber sat again, and while Smith passed out the remainder of the beer, Lucas stood and said, ''Thank you, Captain Gerber. We appreciate your praise.''

Now he slipped into the normal, military speech-making. He talked about the opportunity to carry the war to the enemy and the opportunity to defeat him. They had been fortunate to be able to work with the Green Berets, and if they could be of service again, to call them because they were ready, willing, and able.

After that, the meeting broke up while they finished the end of the beer. Some of the flight crews wandered up to the table to look at the captured material. Gerber made sure that each of them had a chance to take some of the captured North Vietnamese money. Fetterman had already taken them to the arms bunker so they could take a captured weapon apiece, if they wanted it.

Early in the afternoon, they went out to the northern area of the runway, where work parties were already dismantling the revetments for the materials used to build them. There were only three helicopters. The one left in the field had been blown up, and the other, the one that had been shot up so badly, had been airlifted out by Chinook.

Most of the Green Berets were there to watch the flight leave, as a final salute to them. They might not have been trained as infantrymen, and maybe didn't know a lot about survival, but they had been great at what they did. And they were a brave lot.

Even Bromhead was there, although he had to fight with McMillan to get out of the dispensary. He thought it was only right that he be there.

Without much talk, the pilots and crews got their aircraft ready. They cranked, lifted to a hover, and lined up on the runway. Lucas turned so that he could look back and waved once. Then, as one, the flight lifted, climbed out, and turned to the east, heading for Saigon.

When they were gone, Fetterman turned to Gerber. "Now what?"

"What do you mean?"

"Captain, we didn't finish this yet."

"Sure we did. It's all finished. We destroyed the cadre and showed the people that we could protect them."

"But we didn't get the Chinese guy. We've run into him twice and he's gotten away from us twice. Maybe three times."

"You're becoming obsessed with him. Sure, we've run into him a couple of times, but each time, we've beaten him. If the VC had any faith in him, they'll lose it now."

Bocker came out of the commo bunker. "Everything is secure, Captain."

"You get that call to Nha Trang arranged?" Gerber hadn't had time to write to Lieutenant Karen Morrow. He had hoped that she might be with the medical team, but hadn't been. Now, he wanted to tell her that he was in good shape and see how she was. He hoped to get an incountry R and R so that he could visit her soon.

"Lines are down. Maybe later." Bocker headed back to the bunker.

Gerber and Fetterman began to walk toward the team house. Fetterman said, "Think about it, sir. If we could capture him, we'd have a real propaganda coup. The newspapers couldn't keep claiming that this war was an internal struggle between the Vietnamese. We could show them—"

"Forget it, Tony. We have other things to do. Besides, he's got to be in Cambodia by now."

"Then we just forget about him?"

"Did I say that? Did you hear me say that? We'll keep our eyes open. You can talk to Kepler about it, but right now this whole thing is over. We don't need to go stirring up things around here again, until we have a chance to upgrade the training of the strikers. Check on the security for tonight. Have Kepler arrange to have the prisoners picked up.''

''Yes sir.''

''Oh, and have Kepler arrange to get Anh Co Duan into Saigon. We can check with the embassy and see what is available. Surely there will be a position for her there, especially since she can speak English. We can work that through Nha Trang. But that can wait until tomorrow. In fact, most everything can wait until tomorrow.''

''How about patrols?''

Gerber smiled at Fetterman. ''No, Tony, that won't work. I know what you're thinking, but everyone stays in tonight, except for the LPs. I'm going to take a shower.''

With that Gerber moved off, letting his mind slide away from the war, Chinese officers, and Vietnam. He would concentrate on getting clean, but with everything that had happened, he wasn't sure that it was possible. All he could do was try.

GLOSSARY ——————————

AC: An aircraft commander. The pilot in charge of the aircraft.

AK-47: Assault rifle normally used by the North Vietnamese and the Viet Cong.

AO: Area of Operations.

AO DAO: A long, dresslike garment, split up the sides and worn over pants.

ARVN: Army of the Republic of Vietnam. A South Vietnamese soldier. Also known as Marvin Arvin.

BAR: Browning automatic rifle.

BEAUCOUP: Many.

BODY COUNT: The number of enemy killed, wounded, or captured during an operation. Used by Saigon and Washington as a means of measuring progress of the war.

BOOM-BOOM: Term used by the Vietnamese prostitues in selling their product.

C AND C: The Command and Control aircraft that circle overhead to direct the combined air and ground operations.

CARIBOU: Cargo transport plane.

CHEST PROTECTOR: A ceramic plate wore by pilots that is capable of stopping rifle bullets. Also known as a chicken plate.

CHICKEN PLATE: Term used by pilots for the chest protector.

CHIEU HOI: Vietnamese term used to surrender, meaning literally, "open arms."

CHINOOK: Army aviation twin rotor helicopter. A CH-47.

CHOCK: The position of an aircraft in the flight. Chock three would be the third aircraft behind lead.

COLLECTIVE: The control on the helicopter that moves the aircraft up and down.

CREW CHIEF WELL: An area on the UH-1D aircraft where the crew chief sits behind an M-60 machine gun. There is a similar place on the other side of the aircraft for the door gunner.

CYCLIC: The control on a helicopter that moves the aircraft during horizontal flight.

CLAYMORE: An antipersonnel mine that fires 750 steel balls with a lethal range of 50 meters.

DAI UY: Vietnamese army rank the equivalent of captain.

DENSITY ALTITUDE: An aviation term used to describe the thickness of the air when the humidity and temperature are added to the elevation.

DONG: A unit of North Vietnamese money about equal to a penny.

FLARE: Pulling back on the cyclic to lift the nose of the aircraft and slow it down.

FIVE: Radio call sign for the executive officer of a unit.

FNG: A fucking new guy.

FRENCH FORT: A distinctive, triangular-shaped structure built by the hundreds by the French.

GARAND: The M-1 rifle that was replaced by the M-14. Issued to the Vietnamese early in the war.

HE: High-explosive ammunition.

HELLHOLE: An access area underneath the HUEY helicopter that allows mechanics to reach the backside of the transmission.

HOOTCH: Almost any shelter, from temporary to long-term.

HUEY: A UH-1 helicopter.

INCOUNTRY: Term used to refer to American troops operating in South Vietnam. They were all incountry.

INTELLIGENCE: Any information about the enemy operations. It can include troop movements, weapons capabilities, biographies of enemy commanders, and general information about terrain features. It is any information that would be useful in planning a mission.

IP: Initial point. An arbitrary point that signifies the final run-in for a mission.

K-BAR: A type of military combat knife.

KLICK: A thousand meters. A kilometer.

LEAD: The first aircraft in the flight. The flight leader.

LLDB: Luc Luong Dac Biet. The South Vietnamese Special Forces.

LP: Listening post. A position outside the perimeter manned by a couple of people to give advance warning of enemy activity.

LZ: Landing zone.

M-14: Standard rifle of the U.S., eventually replaced by the M-16. It fires the standard NATO round: 7.62 mm.

M-79: A short-barrel, shoulder-fired weapon that fires a 40mm grenade. These can be high explosives, white phosphorus, or canister.

MACV: Military Assistance Command, Vietnam, replaced MAAG in 1964.

MEDIVAC: Also called dustoff—helicopter used to take the wounded to the medical facilities.

NCO: A noncommissioned officer. A noncom. A sergeant.

NINETEEN: The average age of the combat soldier in Vietnam, as opposed to twenty-six in World War II.

NOUC-MAM: A foul-smelling sauce used by the Vietnamese.

NVA: The North Vietnamese Army. Also used to designate a soldier from North Vietnam.

PRC-10: Man portable radio.

PUNGI STAKE: Sharpened bamboo hidden to penetrate the foot, sometimes dipped in feces.

PZ: A pickup zone. An area where the troops or supplies are waiting for pickup by helicopter.

R AND R: Rest and relaxation. The term came to mean a trip outside of Vietnam where the soldier could forget about the war.

RF: Local military forces recruited and employed inside a province. Known as Regional Forces.

RPD: Soviet light machine gun 7.62 mm.

RTO: Radio telephone operator. The radio man of a unit.

RULES OF ENGAGEMENT: The rules that told the American troops when they could fire and when they couldn't. Full suppression means they could fire all the way in on a landing. Normal rules means they could return fire for fire received. Negative suppression means they aren't to shoot back.

SAPPER: An enemy soldier used in demolitions. Uses explosives during attacks.

SIX: Radio call sign for the unit commander.

SKS: Soviet-made carbine.

SMG Submachine gun.

STEEL POT: The standard U.S. Army helmet. The steel pot was the outer, metal cover.

TAI: A Vietnamese ethnic group living in the mountainous regions.

THREE: Radio call sign of the operations officer.

THE WORLD: The United States.

TRAIL: The last aircraft in the flight, responsible for making sure that everyone else is out of the LZ, seeing that the flight is formed, and relaying information to lead, since lead can't see the flight behind him.

TWO: Radio call sign of the intelligence officer.

UH-1D: The D model of the HUEY helicopter.

VC: Viet Cong, called Victor Charlie (phonetic alphabet) or just Charlie.

VIET CONG SAN: The Vietnamese communists. A term in use since 1956.

VNAF: South Vietnamese Air Force.

WILLY PETE: WP, white phosphorus, called smoke rounds.